BLUE MOON

ALANA ALBERTSON

Copyright © 2019 by Alana Albertson

Cover design: Aria Tan of Resplendent Media
Cover Photography: Wander Aguiar
Cover Model: Kaz Van Der Waard

Bolero Books, LLC
11956 Bernardo Plaza Dr. #510
San Diego, CA 92128
www.bolerobooks.com

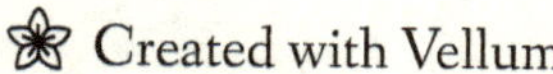 Created with Vellum

Want more romantic reads?

Try my other books!

Rescue Ranch

Navy SEAL Cowboys Series

Wild Love

Meet Chris! She shouldn't fall for the Navy SEAL next door.

Blue Devils

Military Pilots Contemporary Series

Blue Sky

Meet Beckett! I'll never let down my guard for this Devil in a Blue Angel's disguise.

Blue Moon

Meet Sawyer: One Night with this Blue Devil will make you a sinner.

Blue Thunder

Meet Declan: Declan's back in town. Homecoming hero—local boy turned Blue Angel.

Heroes Ever After

Military New Adult Fairy Tale Retellings

The Beauty and The Beast

Inspired by Beauty and The Beast

Meet Grady! But without her love, I'm not a man—I'll remain forever a beast.

The Mermaid and The Triton

Inspired by The Little Mermaid

Meet Erik! I'm a Navy SEAL, a Triton, a god of the sea. And she will never be part of my world.

The Princess & The SEAL

Inspired by The Princess and The Frog

Meet Ryan! She's a Princess and I'm a Frogman. If I kiss her, I'll turn into a Prince.

The Virgin & The Rockstar

Inspired by Rumpelstiltskin

Meet Dax! All she has to do to destroy my life is to say my name.

The Maid & The Marine

Inspired by Cinderella

Meet Trace! I will never be her Prince Charming.

The Swan & The Sergeant

Inspired by The Ugly Duckling

Meet Bret! He was a real man—muscles sculpted from carrying weapons, not from practicing pilates.

Rescue Me

Romantic Comedy Series

Doggy Style

Meet Preston! When it comes to doggy style, he's behind you 100%.

Se7en Deadly SEALs

Navy SEAL Romantic Thriller

Season One:

Conceit, Chronic, Crazed, Carnal, Crave, Consume, Covet

Season One Box Set

Meet Grant! She wants to get wild? I will fulfill her every fantasy.

Season Two:

Smug, Slack, Storm, Seduce, Solicit, Satiate, Spite

Meet Mitch! I'll always be your bad boy.

The Trident Code

Navy SEAL Romantic Suspense Series

Invincible

Meet Pat! I had one chance to put on the cape and be her hero.

Invaluable

Meet Kyle! I'll never win MVP, never get a championship ring, but some heroes don't play games.

Military Contemporary Stand Alones

Badass

Meet Shane! I'm America's cockiest badass.

(co-written with *Linda Barlow*)

Father Figure

Meet Gabriel! Forgive me, Father, for I have sinned.

(Co-written with **Jane Harvey-Berrick**)

I'd like to dedicate this book to my hometown, Marin County, California.

The faults of a superior person are like the sun
and moon. They have their faults, and everyone
sees them; they change and everyone looks up to
them.

— CONFUCIUS

BLUE MOON

ONE NIGHT WITH THIS BLUE DEVIL WILL MAKE YOU A SINNER

Once a year, the Blue Angels perform for Fleet Week in my hometown of San Francisco. They fly over the Golden Gate Bridge wowing the crowds with daring sky stunts and fabulous formations.

Normally, I would just spend the day sunbathing on my rooftop deck. But this time, I'm getting my wings.

As a key influencer, I've been chosen to fly with a Blue Angel.

My heart leaps out of my chest when I meet Sawyer "Huck" Roberts, and it isn't from the G-Force.

This Blue Devil has a girl in every city. Once he finds out I'm a virgin, he refuses to be my one-flight stand. Even so, I'm determined to change his mind.

When he asks me to come with him during his air show tour, I say yes, yes, and oh, yes.

We have nothing in common but cosmic chemistry. I am the sun, and he is the moon. And while the moon chases the sun, they can never be happy together as they're destined to collide only in a total eclipse of the heart.

CHAPTER 1
SAWYER

"**S**awyer, get your ass in here."

I stumbled into the office, my head still pounding from last night's liquor binge. We'd had one of our rare nights off from our insanely packed air show schedule. I'd planned to spend the day sleeping in late at my luxurious hotel suite, golfing at the Presidio, and feasting on dim sum in Chinatown. Hell, maybe I'd even sample all the different types of chocolate down at Ghirardelli Square. Better yet, I'd taste a local woman. But instead, I'd been summoned to base.

I removed my sunglasses and could see my commanding officer Lt. Beckett Daly glaring at me. Puzzled, I stared at his scrunched brow and flared nostrils. Fuck, he was about to hand me my ass, and I didn't have a clue why.

After all, I was the best pilot in the Marine Corps.

But my skills in the air didn't matter. Apparently, I'd royally fucked something up down here on the ground. Again. Maybe one of the chicks I'd hooked up with during our last stop was an admiral's daughter.

Beck just stared at me. Clearly, he wanted me to confess to a crime, but since I didn't know what I'd done, I deflected.

"What's up, man? Congratulations on your engagement again. Tell you what—I'll do your reports today. Go pamper your fiancée."

Beck scowled. "I wish I could, but instead of spoiling her all day, the brass called me at zero six hundred and gave me orders to come in and deal with your shenanigans. Do you mind explaining what this is?"

He thrust his phone at me and showed me a news article. A local television station had mapped out my flight path during practice yesterday.

A flight path in the shape of a dick, complete with balls. A rather large set, I might add.

I laughed it off. "What's the problem? Fucking liberal press. We're pilots—we're supposed to be cocky. Haven't they seen *Top Gun?*"

A vein in Beck's neck bulged, and I was almost certain it would pop.

"Are you high? We're Blue Angels—our job is to recruit and do public relations for the Navy and your beloved Marine Corps. Your stunt was offensive and disrespectful. The command is opening an investigation."

"Fine. Investigate. I'm guilty. It's not like they'll replace me. I'm the only Marine on the squadron. You Navy men are too sensitive." I was a motherfucking Marine. Although technically, the Marines were a Department of the Navy, which we jarheads liked to call "the men's department."

"You're an excellent pilot Sawyer, but you're also a world-class asshole. Do you honestly think women want to look up into the sky and see a giant penis? Especially in this day and age of unsolicited dick pics and toxic masculinity? Can you even see why this is wrong?"

Fuck Beck and his politically correct bullshit. I had better things to do today than listen to him rattle on and on. The only way to get him to shut up would be for me to apologize.

"I'm sorry. What's my punishment?"

Beck tossed me the Key Influencer roster. "You know what you have to do."

Fuck no. Anything but that. "If that's what you want, you can forget it. I'm not taking another one of those vapid, fame-hungry media types up in my plane. I'll write your admin reports for a month, no questions asked. I'll clean your jet and gear. But I won't do that."

The Blue Angels regularly allowed news anchors, local celebrities, and other narcissists to fly around with us on media day. The other pilots didn't mind doing it so I would trade them duties. Media day was a complete nightmare. The last reporter I took up puked all over me when I did a simple inverting trick. And the woman I took before her screamed in my ear the entire trip.

I had to stifle a grin when I thought about her shrieks. "Slow down! Stop! Are you trying to kill me? You're going too fast!"

What could I say? I had the need for speed.

My plane was my temple—there was no room for a wingman.

"I'm not asking you, Sawyer; I'm giving you a direct order." Beck shoved a piece of paper in front of me with a picture of a pretty woman with long black hair attached.

She had a dazzling smile and wore a formal ballgown with a shiny sash that read *Miss Marin County*.

Great. A fucking beauty queen. Sure, she was attractive, but beautiful like a museum piece—looked nice from a distance but too fragile to touch. Definitely not my type. Ladies with proper manners and good upbringings held no appeal for me. I liked my women like I liked my planes—fast, dangerous, and ready to take off and go down on cue.

"Fuck no, Beck. A pageant girl? I'd rather take some old veteran who wants to relive his glory days. Who else you got?"

"We had a veteran on the list, but Declan already claimed him. And I'm taking up the reporter. You don't have a choice. And she's not just a pageant girl, she's an influencer with a huge social media presence. She's documenting a photo series on the Blue Angels. It's one flight, Sawyer. Surely you can be a gentleman for an hour. Then, you can go back to being a jerk."

Man, Beck really hated my guts. He was probably just jealous of my lifestyle. Beck was a family man and his idea of a hot date night was singing nursery rhymes to his baby daughter.

Christ. I was not going to be able to get out of taking this girl up. What the fuck is an influencer anyway? Sounds like another word for lazy millennial. "What does she do for a living?"

"She has a blog and an Instagram account."

I rolled my eyes. "So basically, she doesn't work. And we're feeding into her ego. What's she going to post about us?"

"She pitched it as, 'Her Ride with a Blue Angel.'"

I licked my lips, glanced at the picture, and imagined her naked. Well, I could take her for a ride, but not in my plane. Some things were sacred.

"I refuse."

Beck glared at me.

"Then you're grounded until next week's show. We'll fly without your cocky ass."

"You can't be serious. You will fuck up the diamond formation."

"Well, at least I won't have to worry about you embarrassing us again at the after-show party."

Fuck. He had me. I may love to throw down on my days off, but I loved my job. I lived to fly. Being up in my plane was the best high ever.

I threw my hands up in the air. Time to wave the white flag. "Fine, *Dad.* What do I have to do?"

Beck gave me a smug smile. I wanted to deck the arrogant motherfucker, but he was the flight leader, and there was no use fighting with him. His word was law.

"Easy. You show up tomorrow morning, train her how to breathe during the flight, and then take her up in your plane. Be on your best behavior." He pointed his finger at me. "Which means you need to be polite, gracious, and respectful. She's very media savvy and supposedly will get many eyes on the Blue Angels. We need good publicity, especially after your fucking stunt. There are already protests planned for this weekend. And wear your goddamn uniform when you show up on base to meet her —not your bomber jacket and aviators. You aren't the star of *Top Gun 2.* And you can't hit on her under any circumstances."

Did this motherfucker really think I was that much of a jerk? "Christ, Beck, I'm not that much of a Neanderthal. I *can* speak to a woman without propositioning her; it is possible."

"Could've fooled me. Maybe if you end up liking her, you can invite her to the gala tomorrow night. She looks like a sweet young lady. It would be good for you to spend some time with a woman you didn't meet at a bar. Someone you don't have to pay by the hour. Someone who isn't a Blue Angel groupie."

I smirked. I liked my groupies. I had a girl waiting for me in every city, though I hadn't decided yet who my San Francisco sweetie would be—last year's model or a new ride. Or maybe both—possibly at the same time. The more, the merrier. "Thanks, bro, but I don't need your dating advice. I have zero interest in meeting a nice girl and settling down. That's your whole thing and why you're engaged. You're a serial monogamist, Beck. I'm happy for you and Paloma, but that life isn't for me. I have no desire to have a wife and kids. Ever. I want to live my life and explore the world, no strings attached. But don't you worry, I'll show this girl a good time after the flight. A boring time, but a safe, PC date. Maybe I'll take her mini-golfing, and then we can cap the night off with a hot fudge sundae at Ghirardelli. No nuts. I don't want to scandalize her."

Beck shook his head. "You're a piece of work. A total adrenaline junkie always seeking that next high. Remember this: stable isn't boring, it's beautiful. I'll see you tomorrow for the media flights. You're dismissed. Now get the fuck out of here."

I grabbed the photo of my beauty queen and left the building.

Once outside the hangar, I inhaled a deep breath of the fresh Bay Area air. The weather was brisk and sunny, and there wasn't a single cloud on the horizon. I took a moment to appreciate the beauty of this day and be thankful for my life. A pilot for the Blue Angels. A rock star of the sky. A United States Marine. I wasn't about to let one stupid flight path dick stunt ruin it.

For a poor boy who grew up deep in the Midwest, it always astounded me I'd achieved my dreams.

Pretty good for a kid whose mother said he would never amount to anything. Not that she had a clue about what I had done with my life. If she could see me now, maybe she would feel guilty for how she'd treated me.

How she let all her men treat me. How they—

I closed my eyes and didn't allow my mind to finish that thought. I forced myself to live in the present and shut out my past. Why should I waste time thinking about my mother—I doubt she ever thought about me.

I opened my eyes. I needed something to distract me.

I sat on a bench in the sunlight and stared at the picture on the paper.

Solana Sanchez.

All her relevant information—name, date of birth, phone number, address—was printed on top like a résumé. Solana had recently graduated from Stanford University where she'd majored in psychology and minored in communications. In her free time, she enjoyed taking photos of sunsets and teaching English to recent immigrants.

She sounded like a saint.

But I was only interested in sinners.

I grabbed my phone from my pocket and perused her blog.

Solana Sanchez

Influencer.

Always looking for the sunshine in the darkness.

DM me for collaborations.

I paused over the words "in the darkness." What did this ray of sunshine know about darkness? By scrolling through her Instagram feed on the top of her website, I highly doubted this pampered princess had ever struggled in her life. Selfies in exotic locales and pictures of indulgent dishes and drinks were all she ever seemed to post.

And now she'd use the Blue Angels as another photo opportunity. Riding on our glory and hard work while promoting herself. She couldn't possibly fathom how much I'd sacrificed and overcome to become an Angel.

I should make this hard on her. Do extra flips until she passes out, get her so sick that she pukes all over herself in front of the cameras. That would be hilarious.

Fuck, that's cruel. Maybe Beck is right—I am a dick.

I took a moment and shook off that thought. Nope—not going to humiliate her. That would piss Beck off, and I had no doubt he'd make work hell for me indefinitely if I didn't get back into his good graces. I had to do what he wanted. It was only for an hour, so I just needed to man up and deal with it.

And then I could forget about this sunbeam and go back to planning my wild weekend in the Golden City.

CHAPTER 2
SOLANA

My phone lit up. Thank God! I'd been waiting for this call from my PR agent all day. And what a boring day it had been—I had practiced yoga, spent an hour making the perfect avocado toast garnished with watermelon radishes and microgreens for a flat lay, and then shopped online from some cute dresses in my brand colors of pink, turquoise, and yellow.

"Kelli—did I get it?"

"Yup! The Navy confirmed minutes ago. You've been chosen as a Key Influencer! Congrats, Sol!"

I squealed like a tween at a boy band concert. "Oh my god! Yay me! This is going to be epic. I can't believe I'm going to fly with a Blue Angel."

"I know, right? This is huge. Your followers will freak. I'm working on your hashtag strategy right now. We've committed to four posts, a story, and a live video of you in the plane during the flight. I just hope you don't get sick up there."

A lump formed in my throat. I was already queasy despite still being on solid ground. I didn't like flying when I was in a normal plane, let alone a supersonic jet.

"Ugh. I'm sure I will. What if I puke all over him? I'd die of embarrassment."

"Yeah, that would be humiliating, especially since he's so hot."

My hands shook. "He is? You've seen a picture of him?"

"Yeah, his information is on their website. He's gorgeous. Blond hair, blue eyes, a sexy smile, and a killer body."

Great. Why did he have to be gorgeous? I'd be so distracted and probably start babbling like a moron—I *always* did that around super-hot men. Perhaps one of the many reasons I was still a virgin.

"What's his name?"

"Sawyer Roberts."

Sawyer Roberts, United State Blue Angel Pilot. I'd cyber-stalk him the second I ended this call.

"Got it. So, what's the plan?"

"You'll drive to the base tomorrow morning. I'll email you directions. Please arrive before seven. You'll be briefed on the flight, take a few photos, and then begin your ride. The flight will last forty-five minutes. Once it's over, you'll leave the base. Any questions?"

That didn't sound so bad. Just a short, simple gig. Ha, who was I kidding? I was scared to death.

I exhaled. "No. But I'm petrified. I wish there were a way I could meet the Blue Angels, take pictures, and not have to ride in the plane. More of a lifestyle piece. Wouldn't that be better?"

"Well, your fans would love that, too, but that's not what we agreed to. Maybe you can pitch that to Sawyer after the flight. He might be into it, so long as you don't puke all over him."

Fear gripped my chest. I was all about my image, constantly taking pictures of my supposedly perfect life.

What a joke. If my followers could only see what I actually did on a day to day basis, they'd laugh at me. Maybe this was a bad idea.

"Kelli, I even get carsick. I don't know if I can do this."

"Sol, think of your followers. They will never know what it's like to fly with a Blue Angel. They can live vicariously through you. Do it for them."

She was trying to psych me up, but I still wasn't convinced. I did everything for my followers. My entire life right now consisted of making decisions that were good for them.

"I just hope I don't die from a brain aneurysm. I read about this one woman who died from one after a flight."

"You're so neurotic. You'll be fine. Relax. Honestly, though, you don't have a choice. Your follower count took a nosedive after last month's disastrous collaboration. If you don't shake things up, you'll be yesterday's news."

"I get it." I didn't even want to think about how foolish I was to fall for last month's scam, even though I hadn't been the only influencer who'd been conned. This creeper had fooled Kelli and me. He'd hired a bunch of influencers to take pictures in bikinis for his swimwear line. Then, he started asking for nudes. Of course, I told him to go to hell, but only after I'd already posted the beach shots online, which, of course, he never paid me for. Turns out, he didn't even own a swimsuit line—his accounts and website were all fake. I hated myself for believing he was legit. These days, I couldn't trust anyone was who they said they were.

At least Sawyer was actually a Blue Angel, not some imposter trying to scam me, or even worse, harm me.

"Also, I noticed you have only posted once today. You really need to be posting four times a day. We talked about this, Sol, remember?"

Kelli was such a nag. I used to think she was a friend and that she really liked me, but we never hung out unless it was a work obligation. Frankly, I didn't have any close friends—just collaborators. And I wasn't sure why. After graduation, my friends dispersed, and we'd lost touch. Though I had over one million followers, I felt more alone than ever.

"I know, I'm on it."

"Okay. That's all. Call me if you have any questions."

"Bye."

I hung up the phone, and almost immediately pressure built up in my chest.

Breathe, Sol, breathe.

Speaking to Kelli jolted me into the reality of what I would do tomorrow.

I was going to be flying at the speed of sound.

As an influencer, pleasing people was my job. No one cared whether or not I was happy so long as I *appeared* to be happy. Back in college, I thought it would be so thrilling and glamorous to have a career in social media. Traveling all around the world with no set work schedule; being paid to take pictures and promote products.

But I never imagined how difficult it would be to be "on" all the time. I was definitely not a celebrity, but people still watched my every move. The pressure to be picture perfect was debilitating.

Nor did I realize how dangerous this job could be. I was way too trusting, something I learned the hard way after that creeper had targeted me last month.

And this latest assignment of flying with a daredevil pilot was the most insane gig of all. I'd seen the Blue Angels fly every year since I was a little girl. Those psychos flew their planes inches away from each other, tempting fate. There was no way I could handle that without freaking out. Once, when I took a gondola on a ski run in Lake Tahoe, I had a full-on panic attack. The scorching sun beat down on the hot fiberglass and sweat drenched my clothes. I could barely breathe, and I'd literally thought I would die. Definitely not my idea of a good time.

But this was my job. And, although I hated to admit it, Kelli was right. My engagement with my followers had recently gone down, especially since I'd wasted so much time and energy on that shady collaboration. At least I was back on track professionally, if not emotionally. These images with the Angels should do well, unlike my recent posts. Lately, there had been a backlash against perfect pictures. I guess you could only take so many pictures of lavender lattes and açaí bowls.

Speaking of pictures, time to find one of my pilot.

I entered *Sawyer Roberts Blue Angel* in a quick Google search. Immediately a picture popped up of a blond man in a tight blue flight suit.

I clicked on the picture to get a better view.

Whoa, he was gorgeous.

Eyes the hue of the ocean, sexy scruff on his strong jawline, and muscles that practically bulged out of his flight suit. Were those tattoos on his arms peeking out from the sleeves? He definitely didn't look like the preppy pilot I'd imagined he'd be.

I clicked on his bio on the Blue Angels website.

> Captain Sawyer Roberts is a native of Davenport, Iowa. He attended the United States Naval Academy and graduated with a Bachelor of Science in Aerospace Engineering.
>
> Sawyer reported to NAS Fallon, Nevada, for the U.S. Navy Fighter Weapons School (TOPGUN). Sawyer has flown more than seven hundred combat hours and supported numerous operations and exercises in Afghanistan, Iraq, Syria, and Korea.
>
> Sawyer joined the Blue Angels in September. He has accumulated more than three thousand flight hours and has twenty carrier-landings. His decorations include eight Strike Flight Air Medals, three Navy and Marine Corps Achievement Medals, and various personal and unit awards.

TOPGUN? Like the movie *Top Gun*? This guy was like one of those fantasy heroes who only existed deep in the pages of my romance novels.

I searched the internet for some more intel. I couldn't find any social media accounts under his name. Maybe his accounts were private or under a nickname?

But I scoured the search engines, and still couldn't find anything. Nada. It didn't make sense. I mean, he *had* to have a social media account—what kind of millennial didn't?

I finally found a Blue Angels fan page. And the cover photo was a picture of Sawyer shirtless, drinking a beer on some dock.

Jesus, he had the best body. His chest was massive and covered in tattoos, his arms were ripped, and his abs were rock solid, revealing that perfect *V*. I closed my eyes and imagined those arms wrapped around my body, and my head nestled against his chest. I wanted to lick that man from head to toe.

I opened my eyes and scrolled down the page, thirsty for more.

Bingo.

Holy hell! I wiped the drool from my mouth.

His sexy blond hair skimmed his eyebrows, and his corn-flower-blue eyes melted me. Physically, he was exactly my type—the kind of man I fantasized about every night. Though in reality, I had never dated a bad boy.

I was dying to see how he acted in person.

Well, I would soon find out. I was meeting this handsome blue devil tomorrow morning.

I took another deep breath—I needed to relax.

I walked into the kitchen of my Bay-view condo and filled my teakettle, placed it on the stove, and turned on the heat. As the water slowly boiled, I arranged some blush roses, freshly cut from my small garden, in a golden vase. They would make the perfect Instagram picture.

I paused.

That was the problem with me. Instead of taking the time to smell the roses, these days I waited until they had the perfect bloom so I could take an original picture. I didn't care about their fragrant scent, the unexpected burst of joy I felt when gazing at them, or the overwhelming sense of calm that came over me when I gardened.

For now, my life was all about the picture.

The kettle whistled and jolted me from my introspection. I chose an orange ombré mug I'd bought last week at Home Goods from the cupboard. I hadn't used this cup in a picture before. And once I took a snapshot of my tea, I would probably never use it again.

I placed my loose-leaf chamomile tea in a sun-shaped silicone tea infuser. After I poured the boiling water into my mug, I put it on a tray with the vase of roses in the background.

I snapped a few pictures, edited the best one in my favorite photo app, applied my signature filter, and then posted to my Instagram.

Take a moment for yourself. Hope you all have a beau-tea-ful day!

I added a few emojis, and then copied and pasted my hashtags in the first comment.

#solanasanchez #marincounty #tea #ilovetea #tealovers #tealover #teatime #teacup #sausali- to #teapot #teaaddict #teaparty #teas #teaofinsta-

*gram #teasofinstagram #teastagram #teastory
#marin #marinite #sausalitocalifornia #californiagirl
#afternoontea #teabreak #sausalitoliving #after-
noonteatime #afternoonteaparty #chamomile
#chamomiletea #looseleaftea*

Thank god I had a list of tea hashtags already stored in my phone's notes. I counted again—twenty-nine. I needed one more for the requisite thirty hashtags for maximum visibility.

I paused and looked at the picture. I wanted to hint to my followers what I was going to do tomorrow. So, I added another hashtag:

#onceinabluemoon

There. Posted. *Only two more posts today to go.*

I finally grabbed my mug and took a sip of my tea. The lukewarm liquid was bitter.

Served me right for caring more about the picture of my mug than the warmth or strength of my tea.

I took my tepid, over-brewed drink and sat on my balcony. The views of the picturesque houseboats and the Golden Gate Bridge filled me with joy. Normally, on the week-ends the Blue Angels were in town, I would sit on my balcony and watch the whole show while sipping margaritas and eating guacamole.

But this time I was getting my wings.

Kill me now. I took another sip of tea and prayed the chamomile would calm my nerves. What if I puked on Sawyer tomorrow?

I was certain all the ladies he took up in his plane must swoon over this hunky pilot. A fly-along was the perfect gimmick to meet women.

But with his sexy looks and prestigious job, I was sure he didn't need any tricks. A man that hot probably had a girlfriend anyway or was a complete player. Not that it mattered—he would only be in town for the weekend, and I wasn't interested in having a fall fling.

I gazed out at the bay. It was so beautiful out here. I appreciated this simple moment and was grateful for the freedom my lifestyle afforded me. My parents sacrificed so much in order to send me to the best schools. Now, they spent most of their lives traveling, and I only saw them on vacations. I wished we could be closer. But we weren't. And that was what I was missing in my life. That deep emotional connection. I had no one who was really there for me.

I finished my last drop of tea and said a silent prayer that I would have a safe flight tomorrow.

But as scared as I was, I couldn't wait for morning to come.

CHAPTER 3
SAWYER

I arrived at the base bright and early, ready to accept my punishment. I definitely resented having to take this woman up in my plane.

It wasn't that I was angry about promoting the Blue Angels. I was so proud of who I was and what we did. And I'd have been honored to take up someone who really made a difference in this country—a disabled veteran who fought for our country, a civilian who disarmed a crazed gunman, or a policeman who had risked his life in the line of duty. But not an influencer. I couldn't stand the public's obsession with these nobodies. People who were famous for doing nothing yet were worshipped by the mindless masses. I didn't have Instagram, Facebook, or Twitter accounts. And I never would.

I saw Beck standing in the hangar with our buddy, Declan, the only other single pilot on the squad. But unfortunately for me, Declan was not a good wingman. He was an excellent pilot, no doubt, but he wasn't into picking up random women, though he loved grabbing greasy burgers at dive bars with me. But it was fine that he didn't like to party—I was happy to go solo.

Beck patted my back. "Glad you showed up."

I smirked. "Didn't have much of a choice, now did I? Where is she?"

"She's not here yet."

I turned to Declan. "I'll trade you a beauty queen for a vet."

Declan laughed. "Not a chance, Huck. Besides, the ladies love you."

And that they did. "Fine, I'll take one for the squad."

Beck looked toward the parking lot and suddenly perked up. "And here she is now."

I glanced where he was looking and saw a woman walking toward us.

Solana.

She waved, and I reluctantly waved back.

But when she came into focus, my mouth watered.

I couldn't take my eyes off of her. Damn, she was a complete knockout wearing a bright yellow sweater that hugged her incredible rack. Her shiny black hair cascaded down her shoulders, and I imagined how it would look tangled and wild after sex. Her bright red lips were plump and full, ripe for kissing, and her rocking body filled out her jeans. She had the perfect hourglass figure. Talk about a total bombshell.

She flashed me a big smile and beelined right over to me.

"Hi! You must be Captain Roberts—I'm Solana, but I go by Sol. I'm honored to be chosen to fly with you. I have a big Instagram following and a blog which I will post pictures of this flight on, but I mean, you probably know that. I mean, gosh, I'm such a dork, because you probably read about me in the profile my PR agent sent over. Or maybe you didn't. I don't know what I'm saying. Ugh, I'm sorry. I'm just really nervous and so excited to meet you."

I laughed. She was adorable and surprisingly awkward for how beautiful she was. I needed to ease her nerves. I winked at her. "The pleasure is mine, Sol. You can call me Sawyer."

She said hi to Declan, and then I introduced her to Beck. "Officer Daly, this is Solana Sanchez."

"Nice to meet you, Solana. You're in great hands. Huck is our best pilot."

"Well, it's nice to be reassured. I'm scared to death." Then she looked up at me. "Huck? I thought your name was Sawyer."

I pulled her closer and whispered into her ear, "Huck's my call sign."

"Got it. I've seen *Top Gun.* I know what a call sign is."

I smirked—everyone thought TOPGUN was the ultimate goal for military pilots. I'd been in combat, graduated from TOPGUN, and it had all been a piece of cake compared to the feats I pulled off as an Angel.

A strong gust of wind blew at us, and she dropped her purse. As she bent down to retrieve it, I was graced with an incredible view.

Man, look at that ass.

Nope, Sawyer. Nope. Not this one. Do not hit on this woman.

She straightened back up and bit her nails.

I wanted to hug her and press her banging body against mine, but that was entirely out of the question. What was the proper greeting for a lady? A kiss on the cheek? A high five? Usually, I'd just say, "Let's go back to my hotel." Fuck. I'd lied to Beck. I had no idea how to be a gentleman. Just a jackass.

I took her hand and kissed it like a lovesick sap.

Beck and Declan stepped away and proceeded to laugh their asses off. Cocksuckers. I'd deal with them later.

Sol kept smiling at me, then pursing her lips and looking at her feet. I was used to sexually aggressive women wearing cheap perfume, not shy ones with bubbly smiles who smelled like juicy mangoes.

I stared into her beautiful whiskey-colored eyes, trying to think of something witty to say, but she spoke first.

"I have to admit I'm super scared. I'm not great with heights. Or speed. Or turns. Basically, I'm not good with any form of motion."

I smiled wide and swallowed a laugh. "Well, that's too bad because I'm all about the motion."

A flush crept across her cheeks. "Oh gosh, I'm so sorry. I must sound so stupid. I'm a wreck."

She was nothing like I thought she would be. Based on her pictures, I figured she'd be overly conceited and full of herself. But I didn't get that vibe from her at all. She seemed shy, sweet, and dare I say—innocent.

I dug her.

"Well, don't worry, I'll keep you safe up there. All you have to do is trust me."

I extended my hand to her, and she took it.

"Sounds good. I trust you." She paused and then stared into my eyes. "This may sound silly, but I have a feeling that meeting you will be life-changing."

Oh, one night with me will definitely change your life.

"Oh, it will be, sweetheart. You can count on that."

CHAPTER 4
SOL

Holy hell, Sawyer was fine.

Those pictures I'd seen of him online didn't do him justice.

Handsome was the understatement of the year. He had the best body I'd ever seen. I could see glimpses of tattoos on his muscular arms underneath his uniform. His eyes were mesmerizing, and I legit melted when he winked at me.

But unfortunately for me, I had already made an utter fool of myself in front of him.

I have to admit I'm super scared. I'm not great with heights. Or speed. Or turns. Basically, I'm not good with any form of motion.

I cringed—I was such a dork. I couldn't believe I'd said that.

I started to bite my nails but quickly forced myself to stop because I didn't want to ruin my manicure. There were a ton of other crew members around servicing the planes. One guy had a big checklist, another was doing something to the tires, and one was tinkering with an engine. Why had I agreed to do this again?

As if Sawyer could sense my nervousness, he wrapped his arm around my shoulders. I inhaled his scent—pure testosterone. I was doomed.

"Relax, I got you. You'll be great. Follow me."

He led me into an office and handed me a flight suit. "Put this on over your clothes. Then I'm going to teach you something called the Hick maneuver, so you don't pass out in the jet. Once you master it, we'll fly. I'll be right back." He winked at me again, then left to go to another room.

I went into the bathroom, kicked off my shoes, and pulled the flight suit over my clothes. I quickly freshened up, applied more lipstick and brushed my hair. After I tied my tennis shoes, I left the bathroom.

But Sawyer wasn't back yet.

So, I grabbed my phone and recorded a video. "Hi, everyone. Check out my flight suit. Stay tuned because I will be taking off soon!"

"Damn, you're beautiful."

My heart leaped at his voice, and I stopped my recording. Had my fans heard him say I looked beautiful? They would go nuts.

And forget my fans—did he just openly hit on me? This was supposed to be a professional interaction. Not that it had seemed inappropriate or anything. Hell, I was the one lusting after him. We were two healthy, red-blooded Americans. We clearly couldn't help ourselves.

I turned to find Sawyer standing behind me, holding his helmet and clad in a skin-tight blue flight suit. Warmth pooled between my legs. I'd thought he looked gorgeous in his uniform, but it was nothing compared to how hot he looked now. The tight fabric hugged his ripped chest and arms. I was about to pass out, and it wasn't even from the G-Force.

"You look handsome, too," I managed to say without stuttering. God, I was so pathetic. I could feel my cheeks burning. Why did he have to be so hot?

He placed his arm around my shoulders, and his touch sent tingles throughout my body. "Let's go. I have to teach you how to breathe."

Breathe? I was breathing perfectly fine, thank you. Well, that wasn't true—I was feeling short of breath, but that was only because this man was so gorgeous. "I've been breathing my entire life. What's there to learn?"

He laughed and led me into a small room. When he shut the door, adrenaline rushed through my body. We were alone. A sexy, cocky pilot and an innocent virgin. I wanted him to kiss me, but that would be super inappropriate—not that I would complain. But unfortunately, there was no kissing to be had. Instead, he sat next to me on the sofa.

"So, we don't wear G-Force suits in the planes because they'd interfere with the controls. If you do this breathing maneuver properly, it'll prevent a massive outflow of blood to the brain, and you won't pass out."

Well, when you put it that way, it sounds easy. Not. Oh my gosh! What if I die?

My hands started shaking, but Sawyer reached over and took one in both of his. His hands were warm and should have been soothing, but my nerves were getting the better of me.

"Solana, you'll be fine. I promise."

The way he said my name almost sounded illicit. God, I couldn't concentrate at all.

I didn't respond to him, probably because I was lost in his eyes.

"I'm not going to let anything happen to you."

His words did comfort me. He seemed caring and sweet but looked like the ultimate bad boy with his tattoos and sexy smirk. Was his kindness an act? Or had I really just met my dream man? A gorgeous fighter pilot with a heart of gold had to be too good to be true.

"Okay—so when we go up in the air, I need you to breathe like this." He took a deep breath. "Hick hick hick. Squeeze your thighs, and flex your legs and abs. Do it with me."

I'll be happy to do it with you. Hick, Huck, Fuck.

Damn, where was my mind? Was this a sexual thing or a flying thing? Not that I knew anything about sex or flying. I'd keep my comments and suspicions to myself.

I took a deep breath and squeezed my thighs as tightly as I did in my weekly Pilates class.

"Hick hick hick hick." I sounded like a moron. I looked at Sawyer, who was doing this effortlessly. My eyes focused on his thighs and abs, and I wonder what he would look like naked. He clearly had remarkable control over his body. I bet he was incredible in bed.

Whatever that meant. I was still a virgin. It wasn't a religious thing. I just wanted to be in love with the first person I had sex with. True fairy-tale love. Was that too much to ask for?

Apparently, it was. My college boyfriend had ended up coming out after we broke up. I was so happy for him to embrace his true self, but my joy and support for him didn't ease my heartbreak. And the other men I'd dated at Stanford had all been so self-involved.

I focused my attention back on Sawyer. Even though he had been sweet to me so far, the presence of his tattoos and his overall confidence screamed cocky. Rough, raw, unrefined. Definitely didn't look like one of the mild-mannered gentlemen I usually dated. Not that I had any luck dating sweet guys either. Most of them spooked after a date or two once they realized I recorded our entire courtship for my fans to see. Can't say I blamed them. Dating me was intense.

"Sol, we're going to be going three Gs. I need you to flex those thighs of yours and take a deep breath. Ready, hit it."

He'd paused on the word thighs and was checking me out. Or maybe he was just making sure that I was doing the maneuver correctly. Either way, he was so charming right now. With all the lewd comments, dick pics, and creepy DMs I tended to get from randos on Instagram, it was a welcome change of pace.

I obeyed his orders and took another breath. I was going to take this maneuver seriously because I didn't want to pass out, let alone embarrass myself in front of Sawyer.

After a few more rounds, he finally said I'd practiced enough.

"You ready?"

Nope.

"As ready as I'll ever be," I spoke through clenched teeth.

"You'll do great."

He led me out to a room where the other pilots were waiting.

I posed for some pictures for my required posts. This was a dream job—I couldn't believe I was standing here next to these good-looking men.

Sawyer whispered to me, "Let's go."

I wanted to run away. But instead, I took out my phone and did what I was supposed to do.

I recorded a story.

"Hi, guys! We're going up in the plane right now! Wish me luck."

Sawyer grabbed my phone. "Hi, everyone. We're excited to show you what the Blue Angels can do. Stay tuned."

Wow, he seemed so natural talking to my fans. Maybe he'd be down for doing more stories. I made a mental note to suggest it to him later.

I quickly perused my DMs, and, sure enough, my fans *had* heard him say I was beautiful. My messages were filled with questions asking if he was single, if we were going to date, if we had kissed. Poor Sawyer didn't even know what he had created by that careless statement.

We walked over to the plane, where I took a few more pictures, and then Sawyer helped me into the cockpit. Sawyer caressed the nose of the aircraft, and for a moment, I was jealous of the beautiful blue steel.

There were two cameras in the plane—one pointed at my face and one facing the back of my head so my fans could experience what I was seeing firsthand. As much as I lived my life on camera, this was one experience that I didn't want broadcast, but I didn't have a choice.

Sawyer smiled at me from the cockpit. "Ready, Sol?"

"Yup," I lied.

He strapped me in and then positioned himself. After checking the controls, he spoke into a radio.

"Blue Angel Two to maintain."

I didn't have a clue what he was talking about or who he was talking to, but I didn't want to ask. I took another deep breath and said a prayer.

And off we went—soaring into the sky over San Francisco. The takeoff was smooth, just like a typical plane ride. This wasn't too bad—I could do this.

"We're going to go upside down. Breathe for me."

Just kidding. Get me out of here!

I did my Hick maneuver just like we'd practiced. Hick hick hick, but this was no laughing matter. The blood rushed to my brain, and I couldn't see straight. But that momentary disorientation quickly went away.

"How are you feeling?"

"Good! Never better. This isn't too bad. I could get used to this."

"Great. Now we're getting set up for a loop."

A loop? Is he out of his mind?

"It's going to be three Gs. I need you to breathe with me. Hick hick hick."

I exhaled and squeezed my thighs. Nausea pooled in my stomach, and I could taste bile in my throat. I was going to puke. I reached for the bag.

"All right—how are you feeling?"

I couldn't speak because I was about to vomit so I gave him a thumbs-up.

"You're doing great. Time to go supersonic—take the throttles and push them. We'll be going the speed of sound, which is seven hundred and sixty-seven miles per hour."

Oh my gosh! Why would someone ever want to do this voluntarily? Sawyer must be insane!

A robotic female voice began speaking in the plane. "Warning, warning."

Warning? What did that mean?

"Don't worry about that, it's just something the automated system does. Ignore it, we're fine."

Clearly, we were not fine. Even the plane was warning him to stop.

Save me!

The plane seemed to accelerate at the same pace as my heart. The sudden change in air pressure suffocated me, and I gasped for breath.

But then a sense of euphoria overtook me.

We were floating on top of the clouds. My body felt lighter than air.

"You having fun?"

"Yes! This is incredible."

I couldn't believe how calm and cool he was, not to mention how professional and kind. Seeing this man in his element was incredible.

But my momentary elation quickly evaporated as my head began to pound. I couldn't take it anymore—I puked into the bag, right in front of the camera.

"You okay?"

I nodded yes, but my answer was no. Not okay. Embarrassed, humiliated, ashamed.

"You're doing great. No more tricks. Just relax, and I'll show you your beloved city from a whole other angle."

We flew right over the top of the Golden Gate Bridge, and then he made a sharp right and flew over Alcatraz. Wow. The view really was breathtaking. I'd lived in the Bay Area my entire life but had never seen our beloved landmarks from this mind-blowing perspective.

I could see my reflection in the plane's window. My hair was wild, and I had drool running down my face. My makeup was smeared, and I was downright gross, but by this point, I didn't care.

I was totally in the moment, and I was actually enjoying this flight. I felt weightless and carefree. And completely in awe of Sawyer.

After the longest forty-five minutes of my life, we finally descended.

I did it!

I'd conquered my fears.

Sawyer helped me out of the plane and hugged me. "I'm so proud of you."

"You're fantastic. I'm in awe of you."

He laughed.

I grabbed my phone to record. "Hey, guys. I just had the most incredible plane ride of my life. I'll be uploading it in a bit."

Sawyer spoke to my fans again. "This girl's a champ—she didn't even pass out."

I beamed and turned off the camera. I wanted to freshen up, and then hopefully spend some more time with Sawyer before I had to leave.

As if he could read my mind, he walked me over to the bathroom.

"You can change in there, and I'll meet you in the lobby."

"Okay."

I quickly brushed my teeth, washed my face, and changed out of my clothes. I tried to brush my hair, but it was a tangled mess, especially because a few of my extensions had fallen out. I wrapped my mane into a loose braid and hurried to see Sawyer.

He smiled when he saw me, and I smiled back. Maybe I was reading something into it, or still high from the ride, but I really felt like we were connecting.

He turned to me and gazed into my eyes. "Hey, there's this gala tonight for the Blue Angels. Would you like to be my date? No cameras, though, just you and me."

His date? To a gala no less? A fancy evening where I get to dress up like a princess with a sexy pilot by my side. Umm, hell yeah! Hello, follower count increase!

But ugh, he had said no cameras. He probably meant that he didn't want to film our entire night, but I was sure that he wouldn't mind me shooting a few stories.

Okay, stay cool, Sol. Don't sound too eager.

"I'd like that very much." I hadn't been on a date in a few months. Did anyone even date anymore? I thought they just hooked up. I could never tell if anyone wanted to date me or only grow their own Instagram following. The men with their own followings were the worst. They would slide into my DMs, flatter me with flowers and false promises, and the minute we were Instagram official, they would vanish. Social media prevented people from making genuine connections. There was always another woman to swipe right on so there was no real reason for a man to get to know me.

"Great. I'll pick you up around seven. Here," he handed me his cell. "Add yourself to my contacts, along with your address."

I typed in my information. "Seven is perfect." That gave me plenty of time to shower and change. What was I going to wear?

He placed his arm around me and led me out of the building.

I melted under his touch.

I turned to him and lightly touched his chest. "You were in perfect control of the plane. I couldn't believe it. I'm blown away by you."

He kissed me on my sweaty forehead. "You ain't seen nothing yet."

CHAPTER 5
SAWYER

The gala? I fucking asked Sol to the gala?

I hated going to galas. In fact, I never went. Beck hadn't even ordered me to take her.

Dive bar, I'd meant to say dive bar.

What had gotten into me?

In one word, Sol.

She was breathtaking. Classy. Sweet.

Simply put, totally not my type.

But I wanted her. Badly. When she was breathing rapidly in the plane, I could just imagine her breath hitching as she rode my cock until I made her come.

Something I planned to do later tonight.

I doubted my usual tricks would work on a woman like her.

So, if taking her to the gala would help seduce her, then I was happy to play her game.

Especially since I was so proud of how well she'd done in the air. I'd been certain she was going to pass out, but she hadn't. And she didn't complain once, even after getting sick. I respected that she had been so positive.

I grabbed the keys to my rental, which was a Corvette. I didn't have the luxury of picking up Sol in my Tesla, not that I ever drove it. It was parked on the base back in Pensacola. I was such a transient—different city every weekend. No one to call to check in with every night. No one to miss me when I left. But that was the way I liked it, and the only way I had ever lived. Even when I'd been a kid.

I drove over the Golden Gate Bridge into Marin County and entered the rainbow-painted Robin Williams Tunnel. The Bay Area was spectacular, no doubt. I loved flying here—skimming the top of the bridge, soaring over Alcatraz, and scaring the locals, which was probably why they hated us. Every year, residents protested our visit, saying we were promoting war and luring young men and women to their deaths. What a crock of shit.

The Blue Angels had saved my life. When I was little, seeing them soaring in the sky gave me hope that I could one day have a happy life. I made it my goal to get the hell out of my house and never look back. I studied hard in school and worked my ass off so I could get into the Naval Academy and achieve my dream of becoming a pilot. Being chosen as an Angel was the best thing that had ever happened to me.

I exited in Sausalito and drove down a tree-lined winding road until I arrived at Sol's condo. I parked my car and saw her standing in the driveway, wearing a form-fitting pink dress with a sexy slit right at her thigh.

Damn.

I got out of the car to kiss her on the cheek and then open her door. But before I could say hi, she spoke first.

"Do you mind if I film a quick story before we get going?"

A story? I told her no cameras. Her words immediately jolted me out of my lustful thoughts. Sure, I got that Instagramming was her job, but this was a date, not part of her assignment. Worse yet, she hadn't even greeted me or attempted to have a conversation with me first. Ha, I sounded like a whiny little bitch.

"Whatever you have to do, lady."

She blinked at me rapidly.

Crap. I'd come off like an asshole already—not that I cared. I shouldn't have sarcastically called her "lady." Beck had made me promise to be respectful to her. And maybe I was judging her too quickly. But I wasn't fake, and this morning I'd really thought that there was more to this woman.

"I'm so sorry to ask, but it's my job, you see. If I don't document this, my PR girl will kill me. It won't take long."

Glad to know our date was nothing more than a job to her. I knew filming the flight was her job, but I thought that she actually wanted to go out tonight and have a good time with me. My own horny ass had fallen right into her honeytrap. She just wanted to use me to gain more fans or followers or whatever she called them.

What did she want to film anyway? I could see it now: "My Date with a Blue Angel: How I Gave Him Blue Balls."

She didn't even wait for my response as she whipped out her phone, the latest model iPhone, which had only been released this week. Damn, no trend passed her by.

She stood next to me and pointed the phone toward us.

She grinned a big, fake-ass smile. "Hey, guys! I'm here with Captain Sawyer Roberts, the Blue Angel pilot I flew with today. Now we're going to a gala! Say hi, Sawyer!"

Kill me now. I had definitely made a mistake. Served me right for asking her to the gala. I knew better than to try to go on a date with someone. I needed to stick to late-night booty calls.

Stay in your lane, Sawyer.

"What's up."

She rapidly typed on her phone, inserting hashtags, locations, emojis, and gifs, all the bullshit Instagram crap. I was surprised she didn't put a puppy filter on her face.

Finally, she put her phone away. "Thanks for that. I get that it's annoying, but my followers loved the posts I did earlier today about the Angels. I'm sorry—I'll make it up to you. You look really handsome in that uniform, by the way. You have so many medals." She blushed.

I didn't bother returning her compliment. She already knew she was hot and used it to her advantage. Otherwise, she wouldn't spend her entire life posting selfies. Hell, she probably had a man. She was too beautiful to be single. And she was clearly used to getting her way. Everyone probably bent over backward for her because of her looks. I wasn't going to be one of those guys who fell for her act.

After a few moments in silence, she started talking again.

"Do you like San Francisco?"

I love San Francisco. I just wish I didn't have to spend one of my only days in this city with you. But that's my own damn fault. First for the dick flight path, and then for asking you out. I only have myself to blame.

Aloud I said, "Frisco is great."

She gave me a condescending smile. "Just a tip—no one calls it 'Frisco.'"

Whatever. I'd planned to open the car door for her, but after her story stunt, I decided against it.

I got back inside, and she climbed in next to me.

Damn, why did she have to smell so incredible though? Like a tropical smoothie I wanted to drink down.

She looked around the car and fidgeted.

I glared at her. "Is something wrong?"

"No, I was just wondering if this car had a top."

I rolled my eyes. "Of course, it has a top. Do you have something against convertibles? It's a beautiful night."

"I don't, actually. They're quite fun. But I curled my hair and plan to take more pictures tonight, so if you wouldn't mind, I'd prefer if you put the top up, please."

Talk about high maintenance. This woman definitely wouldn't be up for some wild sex—heaven forbid she got a hair out of place. "Well, lady, if you don't like the wind blowing in your hair, you're with the wrong man. During the flight today, you almost passed out from the G-Force. Your hair was one big rat's nest, and your makeup sweated off, too. Plus, you puked while all your followers watched. Is there a filter for that?"

Her eyes bulged, and she sank into her seat. "It's okay. I understand." She looked away, and her bottom lip quivered.

Ah, fuck. I reluctantly pressed the button for the convertible top.

"Thank you."

"Don't mention it."

She looked hesitant for a second, and then said, "I'm just going to add to my story really quick."

Jesus. She couldn't be off her phone for a minute. This was definitely a mistake.

After exhaling loudly, she primped her hair and smiled.

"We're now heading into San Francisco. DM me your questions for Sawyer."

Who was she? A Kardashian? Who watched this shit anyway?

I'd been wrong about her. She must've been putting on an act at the base. She was exactly who I thought she would be when Beck first showed me her picture. A fake-ass, fame-hungry chick who only used people to get what she wanted. She was fucking smoking hot, no doubt, but any momentary desire I had to seduce this chick went away with her constant filming.

Fuck. I could peace out of this date now, but I didn't want to risk pissing her off and having it come back to bite me in the ass with Beck. So, I would take her to the gala, be civil, drop her back home, and then never see her again.

My hands gripped the steering wheel, and I scowled at her. "Do you always do that?"

"Do what?"

Fuck, it was impossible to hide my disdain. "Record everything that happens to you. Does anyone actually care what you're doing every second of the day?"

She grinned and flashed her phone at me. "Actually, yes. I already have over a thousand views on the first story I posted minutes ago. I searched for you and didn't see any social media. Is your account private? What's your handle? I'll tag you."

Damn, this woman was really getting on my nerves.

"Handle? The only title that matters in my life is my call sign. I spend my life chasing highs, not posting nonsense. You media whores are the worst. I can't believe you get paid for posting about your life."

There. I'd done it. I didn't care what Beck had said. This girl was a spoiled brat. Someone had to put her in her place. And I was happy to be the man to do it.

Her face tensed up, but instead of yelling at me, she flashed me another beautiful smile. "Yeah, I agree with you. I can't believe I get paid for posting either. But I do, and it's my job, and I'm lucky to have it. You may see it as stupid, but for many people, seeing my pictures brightens their day. Also, you're a Blue Angel. Your job is to recruit for the Navy. Maybe a little boy or girl will see my stories about you and become a pilot someday. So, contrary to what you may think, there is some worth and value to my job."

Fuck. She'd actually put me in my place. How long had it been since a woman had done that?

Answer: never.

I exhaled. "It's not just for the Navy. It's for the Marine Corps as well. I'm a Marine. Hence the dress blue uniform."

"Oh, sorry about that. See, this is fascinating. Tell me more."

Do I have to? I just wanted to get this night over with as quickly as possible. To distract myself, I focused on the slit in her dress, exposing her luscious thigh.

"Maybe later, Sol."

She squeezed my hand, and heat jolted to my cock. I accelerated as we entered the highway and took another sideways glance at her.

Sol, I don't blame all your followers for stalking you. We might not have a single thing in common, but you are a goddess. And, by the way, you look fucking incredible in that dress.

CHAPTER 6
SOL

I spent the next stretch of the drive tugging at my locks, winding the strands so tightly, and biting the split ends. My hair was now tangled, which was ridiculous since I'd just given Sawyer a hard time about having the top down. I was so lame. It should have been a fantasy come true to ride in a convertible with a sexy pilot, but here I was, super worried about my curls. I needed to relax and live in the moment.

I stared at the man in the driver's seat. He looked so handsome. His sexy uniform and shiny medals made him look like a prince. His huge hand shifted the gear in the car, and I got wet imagining that same hand controlling my buttons.

Unfortunately, I'd already annoyed Sawyer. He'd been short with me, had called me "lady," and now wouldn't even make eye contact with me, though I caught him checking me out more than a few times. He probably regretted asking me to join him for the gala. He seemed so raw and authentic, and I was as fake as store-bought salsa.

Had I ruined this date already by asking to record a story? How stupid was I? Of course, he was pissed—when he asked me out, he'd even told me that he wanted no cameras. I didn't blame him for being mad at all. I hadn't been thinking—it was second nature to record everything I did. I hadn't realized he'd have such a strong reaction to my request.

I hoped I could turn this night around.

My mind raced, and I tried to come up with something to say. Nothing sounded good, so I turned my attention back to my vice—my phone.

Wow. Two thousand views already! My fans loved Sawyer.

Their messages popped up.

Oh, my god! He's so hot! Is he single?

Good question. I definitely wanted to know about his relationship status. Plus, this would give me a chance to try and smooth things over from earlier. I cleared my throat, and he glanced over at me briefly, arching an eyebrow.

"My fans want to know if you're single."

Fans, Sol, your fans do. You don't care at all, right?

He licked his lips and undressed me with his eyes. "Yeah, as fuck. I don't have relationships. Ever. You?"

I sucked in a breath. I wasn't used to men swearing openly in front of me. I was a virginal pageant girl, proper as a princess. To be sitting next to a man so raw and unrefined rattled me. Even so, he sent my fantasies into overdrive. I bet he was a real-life dirty talker. I'd never dated a man with such a filthy mouth. I was such a good girl, but sometimes I wanted to be bad.

"Yup. I'm focusing on my career right now."

He laughed. Great. He saw my career as a joke. But I expected that, and frankly, I felt like a joke, too. So, I shrugged it off and moved on to the next question.

"Someone wants to know how to become a Blue Angel pilot."

He smirked. "Be the best pilot in the Marine Corps."

Wow, modest much? He had definitely acted nicer back on the base, but maybe that was just because it had been a work obligation. So then why had he asked me out on a date if he'd disliked me? Or maybe he'd been interested after the flight but then changed his mind after I filmed that story. Yeah, I'd totally blown it.

I hate myself.

I typed the answer to my followers and then finally put my phone away. I had to find out if there was a decent man under his cocky exterior.

He eyed me curiously.

"You sure you want to put your phone away? We can mount it on the dashboard so people can see our every move. I can sing songs if they like. In fact, I can even serenade you with 'You've Lost That Loving Feeling.'"

Yes! Do that!

But he was clearly mocking me. I couldn't help feeling a little hurt, but I tried to keep that to myself.

"Funny. But if you're game, that would make a great story. It would go viral for sure. Let's do it." I tried my best to keep my tone lighthearted and fun.

He didn't laugh. This was so awkward. Like one of those Tinder dates from hell where the guy was super-hot, but you had nothing in common. Time to switch gears. "I read you're from Iowa. Do you miss it?"

"Sometimes."

Thanks for the non-answer, buddy. Why was he being so vague? I turned and gazed out the window, rolling my eyes so he couldn't see.

At least we were now driving over the Golden Gate Bridge, so I focused on the view. As we were stopped in the usual bridge traffic, I considered getting out of the car. Not to jump off the bridge or anything crazy, but I could definitely call an Uber to get a ride home. And take an amazing picture of the city at night for my feed.

Focus, Sol.

I tried again.

"I was born and raised in Marin. I love it here. There are so many beautiful places to hike. It's super diverse, too. Weather is usually great, though it can get chilly. Great restaurants, world-class ballet, opera, and symphony. What's not to love?"

He sneered, and his voice turned bitter. "The people. Every year the residents protest our air show—calling us warmongers who spread hate. Claiming we could crash into buildings and kill people, which is ridiculous. Like we're fucking terrorists instead of the people who protect this country. The locals here have no respect for our military."

Well, he was right about one thing—there was a massive protest planned this weekend during the air show. I could see and relate to both viewpoints. Maybe I could help Sawyer understand why they felt the way they did.

"I hear what you're saying, and that must frustrate you, for sure. But the Bay Area is very liberal, and the Blue Angels are a recruiting tool for the military, so that's off-putting to the many residents who want to live in peace and harmony."

Sawyer tightened his grip around the stick shift. Even the beauty of the city lights couldn't distract me from his rage. I could almost feel the heat in his words when he spoke. "Peace? What the fuck do you know about peace? I've been in combat, have you? It's great to live in your delusional little community while the real men and women fight for your freedom to be vapid narcissists on social media. You don't think we'd like peace? That we like risking our lives at war? What should we do when countries are bombing innocent civilians overseas? Or planning terrorist attacks on our soil? There's no such thing as negotiating with terrorists—we've tried talking to them. It doesn't work, lady."

Wow. His disdain for me and my hometown hung thick in the air. I should be livid, but I wasn't. I strongly disagreed with his viewpoint and even more so with his delivery, but my time on the pageant circuit had taught me to kill people with kindness. So that was precisely what I'd do, whether he liked it or not.

"I understand and respect your viewpoint. But Sawyer, just so you know, I'm not a vapid narcissist. I truly care for others, and I give so much of my time to charity. If you got to know me, you'd see that. We can use these photos of the Angels to demonstrate the beauty and honor of what you do to the Bay Area. But the way you're speaking to me, and about my community, will not endear you to them, or me. And frankly, it's unacceptable. I won't tolerate it. If you continue to call me names and cuss at me, I won't even do the rest of the posts I agreed to."

Unsurprisingly, he didn't respond or make eye contact. I bit my lip and willed myself not to cry. I tried so hard to be a good person, and I hated how people saw me. It wasn't just Sawyer; the trolls online were always so intense. Most days, I wanted to delete my profile, move to a mountain cabin, and retreat from the world. But I couldn't quit. This was my job. My life. My sole source of income. I had to deal with the monster I'd created.

We were now driving in the Marina District, and I glanced over at Sawyer a few times. He opened his mouth and looked at me as if he wanted to say something but instead of speaking, just closed it. After a long stretch of silence, he pulled over into a rare open parking space on the street. Sad to say but that parking space was probably the best thing that had happened to me on this date.

"Look, I hate doing the media flights we did today. Normally, I can get out of them, but this time my commanding officer forced me to do it. You seemed really sweet, and of course, you're beautiful, so I asked you to the gala because I wanted to get to know you better. I didn't appreciate you videotaping us when I picked you up. I don't want to sound pathetic, but I felt like you were using the Angels and me. It just set me off."

Videotaped? Oh, he meant when I recorded a story. I didn't want to make this situation worse and explain the difference, because either way, I'd messed up. A lump grew in my throat. Dammit—no wonder he felt used.

Why had I done that? I could totally understand where he was coming from, and I appreciated him being honest with me.

"I'm so sorry, Sawyer. I wasn't even thinking. I usually record my entire day. I wasn't trying to use you. I was really excited about this date, but I totally blew it."

His hand grazed my cheek. "It's cool. I'm sorry I overreacted. I'm very private. I don't even have any social media accounts, so it's hard for me to understand. My entire world is flying, and the Marine Corps is my life, so I tend to lose it when people try to flip the narrative and say we're a bunch of savages. But I shouldn't take that out on you."

"It's okay. I get it. You're a highly decorated military pilot and definitely deserve respect."

"Thank you. And it's not okay. I'm sorry for the way I've been talking to you, Sol. Let me make it up to you."

I pursed my lips and nodded, feeling proud that I stood up for myself and remained calm, even though all I wanted to do was go home, draw myself a hot bath, and cry.

He looked toward a bunch of local shops in the distance. "Hey, do you want to stop and get some coffee before we head to the gala?"

Yes! Coffee! That was just what I needed to take the edge off. Well, a glass of rosé would've been my first choice, but coffee would do for now.

"That sounds perfect. I could use a vanilla latte." *With pretty latte art so I can post a picture.* I smiled at him again and decided to keep that desire to myself.

He opened his car door and then walked over to my side to open mine.

"Thank you." He gave me a cocky grin in return, and I couldn't help blushing.

We walked to a neighborhood coffee shop and ordered. After he paid, his attention focused on something outside, but I couldn't see what it was.

"Hey, I'm going to step out for one second. I'll be right back."

"Okay, I'll wait for our drinks."

Once he was out of sight, I grabbed my phone and made a quick call to Kelli.

"Hey. How's Sawyer? He's gorgeous, especially in that uniform. Your followers are freaking out! Engagement is through the roof."

"He's hot for sure, but I already pissed him off by filming that story of him when he picked me up. And I found out that his commanding officer forced him to take me on the flight today. I'm pretty sure he hates me."

Kelli exhaled. "Oh no, that's unfortunate. I'd assumed since he was an Angel, he'd be *An Officer and A Gentleman*."

I rolled my eyes. Sometimes Kelli could be so cheesy. I preferred that to her nagging though. "Well, he's an officer, but not a gentleman. He's rough around the edges and definitely not what I expected. I wonder what his backstory is."

"Find out and story it."

"No. Not doing that again. He's not into Instagram—he doesn't even have an account. Can you believe that? But I want to find out more about him for myself. He intrigues me. Did I mention he's gorgeous?"

"Yes. Kiss his ass so you can get more photos with him. Make sure to get a bunch of pictures at the gala."

My heart sank. No, I didn't want to do that. I didn't want to use him. "I'll see. Bye."

Our coffees finally arrived, but there was still no sign of Sawyer. Maybe he'd ditched me.

I took a picture of our drinks then carried them to a small table and sat down. Alone. Like I always was. Only a warm beverage to comfort me.

I pressed the mug to my lips and sipped. The sweet vanilla contrasted with the bitter espresso. The warm liquid calmed my nerves, and the caffeine helped to rein in the headache forming.

I'd been so wrong about Sawyer. Earlier today, he'd looked so respectable in his uniform and in his flight suit. If he hadn't opened his mouth, I would have assumed he was a well-mannered gentleman by the look of him.

But I was sorely mistaken.

He was nothing but a devil in an Angel's disguise.

CHAPTER 7
SAWYER

I left Sol standing at the coffee bar with a sad look on her face. Fuck—I'd totally been a dick to her. I needed to do more than just apologize. I headed over to a flower stand across the street.

I'd been an asshole to plenty of women before and never once wasted a second thinking about how I'd hurt their feelings. Why did I care what *this* girl thought? Sure, she was beautiful, but I'd had my pick of gorgeous women once I became an Angel.

Was it because Beck would murder me if I fucked this up? Or was it because Sol was getting inside my head?

Why, why, why?

It had to be because Beck had given me such a hard time about not hitting on her. It was the full forbidden fruit thing—that was why I wanted her so badly.

I could tell by the way her pupils dilated when she looked at me that she wanted me too.

I could still turn this night around.

Maybe we could blow off the gala. And then, I could ask her out on a date to The 500 Club, a historic dive bar in the Mission District. I loved that place. No Instagram-mable drinks that changed color or were served in eggshells. Just good hard liquor. Afterward, I'd take her back to my hotel room and fuck her on the balcony until all of San Francisco could hear her moan in pleasure.

And then, I would never see her again.

Yup. That sounded like the perfect plan.

Fuck Beck and his bullshit relationship talk. That life was right for him, but it wasn't for everyone, and most certainly not for me. I knew who I was. I liked who I was, and nobody was going to change me. Not even this gorgeous pageant queen.

I picked up the phone and called Beck to check in since we would be missing the gala. He answered on the first ring.

"Hello? Am I your one call?"

"Funny. No, I didn't get arrested."

"What's up, man? Did you piss Solana off? Is she not coming to the gala tonight?"

How did he know? "Fuck, man. Is that what you think of me? A total fuck- up?"

"Yup. You're an ace in the air, but sometimes I wonder how you graduated from Annapolis. You know, I fought for you to get on this squad—the other guys didn't want another cocky pilot, but I swore you'd come through for me. I believed in you and was impressed by everything you overcame to get here. I still am. Don't make me regret my decision."

I paused. I never knew Beck had been the one to endorse me through the audition process. It was so hard to become an Angel. Only six pilots were on the squadron, and only three new pilots were chosen each year. The audition process was brutal. I hoped we found some cool dudes this year—in fact, I'd make sure of it.

I needed to clean up my act. Getting kicked off the squad would be the worst thing that had ever happened to me, which said a lot, considering the fucked-up childhood I'd had. I would never forgive myself if I ended up being replaced due to my behavior on land. I needed to be a better man.

"Well, I'm going to come through for you. Though we won't be going to the gala."

"Why are you calling me? The gala isn't required, though you should attend, so the brass sees you're making an effort to behave. Do you want to ask me something? Advice maybe? Or do you need to get a confession off your chest?"

I swear that dude could see right through me. "I guess. When I picked her up, I was pretty fucking annoyed by her. She was recording our every second for her Instagram and didn't even bother talking to me at first. So, I kind of lost it. Went off on her for her lifestyle and living in this city. I was a jerk."

Beck let out a long sigh. "Huck, you didn't. I told you—"

"Yup, I know you did. After I said those things, I knew I had completely blown it with her. She seemed genuinely hurt, and I felt awful. Shit, I still feel awful, I do. But instead of yelling at me, she calmly put me in my place. She pretty much told me that I was an asshole. But then, she said she respected my job. I know this sounds stupid, but I feel like she really understands me."

"Dude, you need a therapist, but I've told you that before. Do you want my advice?"

"Nope," I lied.

"Too bad—I'm going to give it to you anyway. Instead of trying to get Sol into bed, just get to know her as a human being, not as a sex object to be used for your pleasure. Feel what it's like to spend some time with a woman without your typical end game. You could surprise yourself."

That sounded like hell. Why would I spend time with a woman if I wasn't going to get laid? If I wanted to hang out with a friend, I'd chill with Declan. I knew him, I trusted him, and he always had my back. He was my legit wingman.

But Beck's idea latched onto my brain like a leech. "I'll think about it."

"Where is she now? Where are you?"

I grabbed a bouquet of flowers from the stand and handed the lady two twenties. "Buying her flowers."

The lady smiled and tried to hand me my change, but I waved her off as I turned to look back at the coffee bar. Sol was sitting by herself at a table with our drinks, and I didn't want to keep her waiting any longer.

"Nice save. Seriously, be good to Sol. That's an order."

"Yes, sir. Got it. I'll text you later."

"Later, bro."

I walked back to the coffeehouse. Sol gave me a big smile when she saw the flowers in my hand. My chest swelled with pride—I was glad I could make her feel better after the crappy way I'd treated her.

I just hoped I hadn't already fucked up this night beyond repair.

CHAPTER 8
SOL

Sawyer was walking toward the coffee shop, holding a bunch of red and yellow sunflowers. My heart raced. How sweet. I couldn't remember the last time a man had given me flowers.

He stepped inside with a sheepish grin and sat down across from me at my table.

"These are for you."

Swoon! "Thank you! They're gorgeous. Sunflowers are my favorite. I buy them every week at the farmers' market."

Damn. Why did this have to be such a great Instagram worthy pic though? I could arrange them out right next to our coffees, and there was even a neon quote on the wall that would make the perfect background.

Do not take a picture, Sol.

He smirked. "I know. They were all over your Instagram."

Ha! He had been looking at my feed? I tried to play it cool and tease him a little.

"So, you *do* have an Instagram? I thought it was just for us vapid narcissists."

"No, I don't. Your pictures are on your website."

Right. "Cool. I can hardly believe you don't have an Instagram though. Everyone has one. How do you keep up with your friends?"

He looked me dead in the eyes, a now serious expression washing over his face. "All my friends are on my squad. I go drinking with them, or we play golf. Or if it's one of the men I served with in combat, I call them when I stop by their city. I don't have the desire to keep in touch with people I don't have time for in real life."

Wow. His words hit me like a punch in my gut. I didn't know anyone who lived like that these days. "That's cool. I wish I could be more like you." His life made sense and seemed super healthy. What would it be like to live like that? Not that I was going to try it any time soon.

"You're a sweet girl just the way you are, Sol. I promise I'll treat you well for the rest of the night assuming you still want to spend some time with me. But honestly, I really don't want to attend the gala."

I pursed my lips. I was a little bummed about not attending the gala—I had harbored some fantasy of dancing the night away with Sawyer. I did want to spend more time with him, but by now my head was spinning. I couldn't believe I was actually going to end this night early. "Thanks for that. I'd love to hang out with you, though I'll be honest, I'm not feeling too well. I think I'm still a bit nauseous from the flight, and I'm getting a headache. It's just been a long day."

He sighed and honestly looked disappointed, which made me feel good knowing that he at least wanted to spend time with me. "I understand. Flying like that takes a toll on your body, especially the first time."

I paused over the words "the first time." He was talking about the flight for sure, but maybe he could tell I was a virgin by the way I acted. That was doubtful, but I always feared that I gave off an obviously inexperienced vibe.

I touched his knee. "Can I get a rain check?"

He looked into my eyes and smiled. "Sure, are you free tomorrow night? I'm only in town until Monday morning."

Right. And tonight was Friday. At best we only had two more nights together.

"Yes, I'd love to. But there is one condition."

"What's that?"

"Let me pick the place—I want to show you San Francisco. And wear a suit. You'll fall in love with my city."

He took a sip of his espresso. "I'm game—it is one of my favorite cities to fly in. Let's get out of here, and I'll take you home."

"Sounds great."

We finished our coffee and walked out of the shop. The night was chilly, and the fog was low, almost creating a mist over the city. It was incredibly romantic.

Sawyer opened the car door for me and drove me home. This time the drive didn't feel awkward at all, although I wasn't up to doing a lot of talking because of my headache.

When we arrived back at my place, he walked me to my door. I considered inviting him in but decided against it. I didn't want to send him mixed signals since I had no intention of sleeping with him, because, let's face it, I was stupid. Any other woman in her right mind would lead this sexy man straight into her bedroom. But I never acted on my impulses and desires.

"Good night, Sol. I have the air show tomorrow in the afternoon, but I can come by and pick you up around seven."

The air show. I couldn't wait to see him fly, but I had VIP tickets for the Sunday performance. At least I could watch him tomorrow from my balcony.

"Sounds great. Looking forward to seeing you tomorrow night, and I can't wait to watch you fly on Sunday."

Sawyer kissed me on my cheek before walking off into the moonlight.

***

I woke the next morning feeling excellent! Super bright and energetic. And thankfully, my headache was gone.

As much as I wanted to watch Sawyer fly, I decided to wait until I was at the air show so I could get the full experience. Even so, I could hear the jets passing above my place.

After spending a leisurely afternoon lounging around my place, I finally got ready for our date. And unlike the anxiety I had last night, I was looking forward to it. Sawyer and I had really turned a corner, and I knew we would have a great time tonight.

What would I wear? I checked the forecast—another foggy fall night. I had to dress warmly.

I perused my closet, filled with bright dresses that were on brand for me, but inappropriate for the restaurant I was taking Sawyer to.

Next, I inspected my business suits. Nope. Too formal. This was a date.

I studied the rest of my clothes. Maybe I should wear a button-up shirt and slacks.

I picked one blouse and eyed it critically—it didn't spark joy, so I threw it into a donation box that was hungry for items. I seriously needed to declutter my closet, and soon, since it was packed with so many clothes that had been gifted to me that I'd never wear. I'd been super inspired since I saw a documentary about organization on Netflix.

Maybe I could pitch a decluttering challenge to my PR company and get it sponsored?

Man, why couldn't I focus? Clothes! Date! Tonight!

After a few more minutes, I finally found what I was looking for.

The perfect outfit, one I hoped Sawyer would appreciate. It wasn't even in one of my brand colors. Kelli would murder me.

It was a simple black cocktail dress. I slipped off my shirt and sweatpants and pulled the dress over my head, the soft fabric caressing my curves.

One look in the mirror and I knew it was exactly what I wanted. Flattering but not tacky. Classy and elegant, with a hint of sex appeal. Not too eager, not too standoffish. Yay!

Now for the shoes.

My eyes gravitated toward a pair of pink high heels. Was that too much? The bright pink shade would pair well with a nice glossy lipstick. I'd change out of the heels if I could convince him to go with me after dinner to look at the Blue Moon. But this outfit was perfect for a date with Sawyer.

I couldn't wait for him to pick me up.

CHAPTER 9
SAWYER

After a perfect air show, I got ready for our date. I took my time, showering and shaving before getting dressed. Then I massaged in some after-shave and took a final look in the mirror. I was used to wearing my dress blues with all my medals or my flight suit, but these designer threads were foreign to my body. I couldn't even remember the last time I'd worn a suit and tie. I saw myself always as a Marine—first to fight, last to leave. But that was the problem. My identity was entirely tied to my job. Blue Angel, fighter pilot, Marine. Sometimes I didn't know who I was outside of work. And putting on this monkey suit stripped me of my work identity. It also covered my tattoos and scars. I looked like a businessman. A businessman who was about to go on a date with a beauty queen. Wasn't that a joke.

When I arrived at Sol's place, she was already waiting outside, wearing the sexiest black dress. Damn, she really was a knockout. I wanted her so badly. Right now. But I would be patient and wait until after dinner—she would be my dessert.

I got out of my car and opened the door for her. This was way too formal—we were dressed up and going to dinner in the city. This was most certainly a date. And I never went on dates.

All day I couldn't stop thinking about Sol. I was dying to eat her pussy, fuck her from behind while slapping that phenomenal ass as she screamed my name.

Fuck Beck and his spend some time getting to know her bullshit. This was a hot weekend fling. All it could ever be. All I wanted it to be.

Yup, I had to have her. Tonight, she would be mine.

The wind blew up her dress, and I hoped to get a glimpse of her panties but had no such luck.

I kissed her cheek, though I wanted to plant one on her lips. Not yet though. Our first kiss would be epic—one for the books. "You look beautiful, babe. Where we headed?"

"Do you like seafood? There's this amazing Chinese restaurant. Their salt-and-pepper crab is to die for."

Now we were talking. I'd been eating nothing but the same catered crap for weeks.

"Sounds great. Which way?"

"The city."

Once we went over the bridge, she directed me through the maze of San Francisco traffic. Who designed this city? There were so many one-way streets, it was a mess. But I sucked it up for our date and kept my thoughts to myself. Luckily, the only traffic I normally had to deal with was air traffic.

We finally arrived at the Embarcadero, and I left my car with the valet. Once outside the car, I saw a long line of people wrapped around the building.

I hated crowds. "Do we have a reservation?"

She shook her head. "Not exactly."

Nope. Not going to happen. I don't do trendy hot spots.

I didn't want to spend my night waiting like cattle when I could be feasting on food. And her. I still hoped I could convince her to go to that dive bar with me after dinner and then back to my hotel. I had to keep this night moving.

"The wait looks pretty long. Let's find something else."

She smiled. "Follow me."

I gladly let her take the lead while I walked behind her and stared at her incredible ass. I couldn't make out any panty lines. Was she wearing a thong? I'd find out later tonight when I undressed her.

Sol walked up to the hostess, who embraced her and then immediately showed us to a table.

What the . . .

We sat down at the lone empty booth in the back, which had an incredible view. Sol cuddled up next to me, so I put my arm around her and whispered into her ear, "Do you know the owner or something?"

"I mean, not personally, but I've been here before, and my Instagram is well-known. If I post a picture of their dishes, they'll get tons of free publicity."

Got it. I was starting to see the perks of her job. "So, where's the menu?"

"Oh, that's the catch. They'll serve us what they want me to feature, usually their in-season specials. But they'll bring the crab dish for sure—it's their signature dish. Everything will be delicious, I promise."

Wow. Okay. I didn't like my choice of entree being taken away, but I wasn't going to complain. "Can I order a beer, or do they decide what I want to drink, too?"

Before she could answer, the waiter brought over a bottle of white wine. So much for the Tsingtao beer I craved. After the waiter poured me a sip of the wine to taste, I okayed it, and he filled Sol's glass and mine. Then, Sol took a picture of the wine label.

"I'm going to do a quick story."

"Knock yourself out, babe." I still wasn't used to her phone addiction, but I was hungry and horny, so I didn't care at this point. Her eyes were hypnotic, and her bright pink lipstick contrasted with her skin, which was the color of the harvest moon. She really was stunning. But I wasn't just physically attracted to her. I was impressed that she was financially independent, even if her job seemed pretty superficial to me. I'd met many women who wanted to marry men in the military just so they could get free benefits, but that definitely wasn't the case with her. Hell,

Sol probably made more money than I did, which pissed me off.

She positioned her phone in front of her face. "Hey! So, we're at Harborview Restaurant and Bar in the Embarcadero." She turned her phone toward me.

Fine, I'll play.

I waved. "What's up? I'm Sawyer—a Blue Angel pilot. Come out and see our show tomorrow. Now, if you'll excuse me, I want to get back to my beautiful date."

Sol's face lit up at my words. She turned the phone back towards her heart-shaped face and continued, "Check back to see what we have for dinner."

I turned my attention to the incredible view outside the ferry building. I had a blast flying today at the air show. Sol had only experienced a few of my tricks in the plane— I couldn't wait for her to see me fly with my squadron.

Our first appetizer came, which the waiter informed us was Kurobuta Pork Xiao Long Bao, which consisted of these small dumplings set in a bamboo steamer. I'd tried this dish before in Chicago and loved it. I used my chopsticks to place one of the steamed dumplings on my spoon, but Sol gave me a dirty look.

"Wait one second, please. I need to take a picture."

Oops, too late. I'd already popped that little sucker into my mouth. I bit into the dumpling and my taste buds danced, relishing the mix of the tangy broth and impossibly tender meat. I'd never tasted Chinese food like this before. No wonder Sol loved the culture of this city.

"Sorry about that. These are amazing."

She gave me a reluctant smile and put down her phone.

I studied her face as she chewed. She had a sexy mouth, and I loved her long flowy hair. She was definitely a perfect ten.

My eyes dropped to her legs. I was grateful she was seated next to me in this booth so I could stare at her entire body without being too obvious. I wanted to touch her tan flesh and lick her all the way down to her fuck-me heels. I planned to do just that later tonight.

Damn. If I wanted to seduce her, I'd better start talking to her before another dish came, and she ignored me to take more pictures.

"So, babe, tell me more about yourself. What do you like to do for fun?"

She gave me a blank stare. "Fun? Most of my fun is sponsored and scheduled. But I like to go hiking in Muir Woods. And I love the opera and the ballet. How about you?"

Well, at least we both liked hiking because I wouldn't be caught dead inside a theater. "Anything outdoors. Sky diving, rappelling, BASE jumping, boating."

"So . . . you're a thrill-seeker. I mean I guessed that by your job choice. Why is that? Do you ever like to just chill?"

Chill? What was that?

The truth was that nothing sounded more awful to me than sitting around and doing nothing. I liked to keep my mind and body active, that way I didn't start reliving my past. But I wasn't going to tell her that.

"I'll chill with you." I gazed into her eyes and whispered into her ear. "Hey, this restaurant is great, but I need a change of pace. After dinner, let's stop by my favorite dive bar, get a few more drinks, maybe play some pool. And then, we can head to my hotel room— it has a great view of the city. We can drink some champagne and get to know each other."

She let out a nervous laugh and pulled away from me. "That sounds great and all, but I was hoping we could go see the Blue Moon. There's a great view on the top of Mount Tam."

Great. That sounded *romantic*, and romance definitely wasn't my thing. But I was never one to say no to adventure, and I loved being outdoors. Maybe I could fuck her on top of the mountain, under the moonlight. I smiled and nodded.

"Sounds like a plan."

A few more dishes came, including the crab. She was right —it was delicious, and I savored every bite as I had my fill. I was ready for dessert, and by that, I meant feasting on Sol's luscious curves.

Finally, she confidently flipped back her hair. "Let's get out of here."

CHAPTER 10
SOL

Sawyer licked his lower lip and signaled to the waiter. "Check, please."

I let out another nervous laugh. "Sawyer, the meal is free."

He fidgeted in his chair and slapped down a hundred-dollar bill. "Well, I'm going to at least give them a tip. And babe, nothing in life is free."

His words caught me off guard. He was so right. Nothing was free. Though I dined in fancy restaurants, stayed in luxurious hotels, and was regularly invited to exclusive events, everything came at a cost. I wasn't free to be truly honest with my opinions—I always gave my sponsors glowing reviews. Was that unethical? My followers hung on my recommendations and went places that I frequented. Didn't my fans realize that my opinions were influenced? That was my legit job title—influencer.

A chill overtook me. I hated thinking about this fake persona that surrounded me. I constantly justified it to myself, but after only knowing Sawyer for two days, I was already questioning how I lived my life.

"Let's go." He grabbed my hand, and we left the restaurant.

As we waited for the car, I leaned into him and inhaled his earthy scent. He smelled so good, like a combination of cedar and mint.

He wrapped his arms around me, and I thought for a second that he was going to kiss me, but instead, he put his thumb under my chin and forced me to look at him. "You're breathtaking, Sol."

My lips widened into a smile. Last night had been so awkward, but now I could sense this big shift in his personality—he actually seemed interested in doing what I wanted to do.

Well, I'd take advantage of his gentlemanly behavior for as long as it lasted.

The valet pulled up with the car and handed the keys to Sawyer, who opened the door for me. Then, Sawyer tipped the guy and off we went on our next adventure.

I directed Sawyer back over the bridge—as much as I loved San Francisco, Marin County was my hometown.

As we exited in Mill Valley, he pulled in front of a drug store. "I'm going to stop here really quick. Do you need anything? Or do you want to come in with me?"

Honestly, I had to update my Instagram story, something I would prefer to do in private since clearly it bothered him. "No, I'm fine in the car. But if you could just get me a bottle of water, that would be great."

"Sure thing." He kissed my cheek. "I'll be right back."

Once he was inside the building, I grabbed my phone and hit record.

"Hi, guys. We just finished with dinner, and now, we're heading up to the top of Mount Tam to catch the Blue Moon." I quickly posted the story and counted the minutes until Sawyer returned to the car. Suddenly, I was more interested in spending time with him than on my phone. I hadn't felt like this about anyone in a while. Sawyer was so confident and in control, which I found quite sexy. Plus, his occupation was so elite. It seemed like the only men I'd met recently either worked in tech startups, were influencers, or were trust fund babies. Sawyer was a welcome change.

He finally emerged from the store, carrying two bottles of water and a blanket.

Nice job, buddy.

He threw the blanket in the backseat and handed me my bottle of water. "Here you go."

"Thank you." He backed out of the parking lot and started driving up the mountain as I opened the bottle and took a sip. I also kicked off my heels and changed into a pair of foldable flats I'd tucked away in my purse.

I could feel my heart racing. I was about to go somewhere isolated with a man I barely knew. Sure, he was a highly decorated pilot, but I still didn't know anything about him. Who was he? What was his family like? What did he want out of life?

As if he could sense my anxiety, he reached over and placed his hand on mine. "You okay?"

"Yup. Just nervous, that's all." About tonight. We'd had a good date so far—what if he expected sex? He *had* tried to get me to go to his hotel room. Luckily, he didn't make me feel uncomfortable or give me a bad vibe. Honestly, he made me feel safe. Ever since he'd brought me flowers last night, he had gone out of his way to treat me well. But even so, I was worried about telling him I was a virgin if the night progressed.

"Why are you nervous?"

I shrugged. "I just . . . I don't know. I don't date much."

"Neither do I."

That wasn't reassuring. Of course, he didn't date much—he was a player. This man had women throwing themselves at him in every city. And apparently, I was one of them.

I exhaled.

Sawyer squeezed my hand. "Relax, babe. We're just going to stargaze. I'll behave like a perfect gentleman."

And with those words, a sense of calm washed over me. I couldn't figure out Sawyer. Was this sweet man his true persona or was he really the cocky jerk from the other day? Maybe he was just the best smooth talker ever.

I decided to call him out.

"You know, you try to act all street-smart and rough, but you aren't like that at all. You're actually sweet and kind."

He laughed. "Are you saying *I'm* fake?"

"No. I'm not. I'm just trying to figure out who you are. What you stand for."

"Here's a tip, babe. Stop trying. What you see is what you get."

Right. It was stupid of me to try and psychoanalyze him. I just needed to relax and live in this moment.

I gazed at the stars for the rest of our journey. We lapsed into a comfortable silence before we finally arrived at the small parking lot. He grabbed the blanket, opened the door for me, and led me by the hand up the popular trail I'd been exploring since I was a child.

After we arrived at a beautiful clearing with a good view of the moon, he spread out the blanket, and we both sat on top of it.

He pulled me into his arms, close enough that I could see our breaths commingling in the air. "I used to stargaze all the time back home."

Yes, he was finally opening up to me. I was desperate to know more about him, details that weren't on the Blue Angels website.

"In Iowa?"

"Yeah. My buddies and I would head up to the Eden Valley Refuge when we could—go hiking and camping. We'd go to the observation tower and look at the stars."

"That sounds amazing. I've never been to Iowa. Do you like it?"

"Yeah, but it was cold in the winter. Good people, though. Real. Honest. Hardworking. How about your friends?"

Friends, what were those? I only had followers. "Well, I'm not close to my college friends anymore. And my family travels all the time, so I rarely see them. The only person I really talk to is Kelli, my PR agent."

He tilted his head and made intense eye contact. "That sounds lonely. At least I always have my fellow pilots."

Ugh, he was so right. I *was* lonely despite having all my followers on Instagram. A million followers and not a single one knew the real me.

But enough about me, I wanted to know more about him.

"Do you have a big family back there?"

"Nope."

He quickly shut down the subject of his family. I wanted to ask more questions but didn't want to pry. Sawyer obviously valued his privacy, and I wanted to respect that.

His gaze turned to the moon, big and beautiful, tinged with a hint of blue. "Do you know what makes the moon appear blue?"

"No. Do you?"

"Yeah. I learned about it at Annapolis. The moon appears blue when the atmosphere is filled with dust or smoke particles, which scatter red light. This moon is probably blue because of the recent forest fires up north."

My heart sank. So much devastation in my state. So many California residents had lost their homes, and an entire town had been pretty much wiped out.

"I didn't know that. You must be brilliant to be a pilot."

He grinned. "And you must be really smart to have graduated from Stanford. And to have built your following to millions. Though I'm sure everyone follows you because you're so beautiful. If I had an Instagram, I'd stalk you."

His hand cupped my face, and he pulled me into him. My heart was beating faster than it had ever before. He was going to kiss me. Did I want him to? Sure, I'd fantasized about him fucking me, but that wasn't even realistic. I was not going to lose my virginity to a man I would never see again. But kissing this man under the Blue Moon struck me like something deeper. Something more intimate. Something scary.

I closed my eyes and gave myself over to the moment. Our moment. His lips touched mine, and the scrape of his stubble scratched my chin. I opened my mouth as his hot tongue penetrated mine. Softly at first, but quickly turning rough. Hunger grew inside me, and I kissed him back, desire seeping through my pores as I ran my hands along his body. This was a kiss to end all kisses. He tasted like warm wine and lust. Forbidden yet so inviting. Passionate but loving. And none of those contradictions, those feelings, those thoughts made any sense. This was just a kiss in the moonlight with a man who would never be anything more than a casual fling. A man who I would probably never see again after the end of this weekend, or if I did, only be once in a Blue Moon.

I finally summoned the strength to pull away from him. I opened my eyes to find him staring at me expectantly.

I didn't know what to say, so I turned my attention to the moon. "Wow, this moon is so stunning. Thanks for coming up here with me."

"Thanks for taking me out here. I had a good time with you tonight." He looked at his watch. "We should be going soon though. I'll drop you off at home and then head back to my hotel. I have to get up early for tomorrow's air show."

Right. Wow, I was shocked that he wasn't even trying to spend the night with me. Maybe I had read him all wrong. I'd callously assumed this bad boy pilot was just some womanizer with low morals and a high libido.

"I understand. Let's go."

We stood up, and he folded the blanket. After walking back to the parking lot, we got into his car, and he drove down the mountain back to my place. He pulled in a guest parking space before getting out of the car to open my car door for me. Still a total gentleman. Swoon!

"Let me walk you in."

I nodded and led him to my front door. Would he try to come in? Kiss me again? Shake my hand? Maybe he wasn't attracted to me or thought I was a horrible kisser. I pulled at my hair as anxiety crept up inside my chest.

"Well, this is me. Do you want to come in and have some tea?"

Tea? As if. Whiskey, Sol, not tea.

"Not tonight, babe. I'm gonna call it."

I pursed my lips and tried to blink back the disappointment. Why did I care? I'd practically hated him yesterday. Apart from his undeniably good looks, he had been rude and arrogant. He didn't live near me, and we could never ever be anything more than a fling.

But something about him, like the way he'd treated me during the flight and on our date tonight, made me believe deep down, Sawyer was truly a good man. He was real and honest and caring like he'd described his friends back in Iowa. Something must've happened to him in his past that had forced him to wear that cocky exterior like armor.

But in our limited time together, I would never have the opportunity to get to know him.

"Okay, night." I debated giving him a high five, then turned to the door and fumbled with my key.

He twirled me around by the wrist, pressed me up against the door, and kissed me again. But this kiss wasn't like our first—it was full of lust, and I could feel his hard cock press against me. His left hand gripped my thigh as he hiked up my dress, and his tongue darted into my mouth.

Oh my god! I was melting against him. A hunger I had never experienced bolted through my body.

This time, he pulled away first and gave me a devilish grin.

I caught my breath, and my cheeks burned impossibly hot.

"Night, Sol. I had a great time tonight. Thanks for taking me to the restaurant and to see the Blue Moon. After the show tomorrow, I'm taking you on another date. But not to one of your fancy Instagram-worthy five-star restaurants. We're going to a dive bar."

Dive bar? I wouldn't be caught dead in a dive bar. What would I post?

I opened my mouth to say as much, but was shocked to hear myself reply, "I can't wait."

What was wrong with me? Two kisses from this hunk and I was acting completely off-brand. Like a different woman.

The scary thing was I liked it.

CHAPTER 11
SAWYER

I couldn't believe I hadn't even tried to spend the night with her. That was a first. What the fuck was wrong with me? I was losing my edge.

It wasn't that I didn't want to. No, definitely not that. Kissing her was incredible. She tasted just as I imagined she would—sweet and spicy. Her hands were so soft and delicate when they traced my face, but all I could imagine was her nails scratching my back as I fucked her. So why hadn't I even tried to close the deal?

Was I developing feelings for her?

No, that made no sense. Feelings weren't my thing. Lust was more my deal for sure. I'd never truly cared about any woman I'd been with. I'd have a great one-night stand and then say goodbye. That way no one got hurt.

Sol wasn't even a girl I could ever date, even if I did want a relationship, which I most certainly didn't. Unlike Beck's fiancée Paloma, who hadn't had a job before she met Beck who hired her as his daughter's nanny, Sol had an entire life here in the Bay Area. Her Instagram name was @SolanaSanFrancisco. She lived in a part of the country that I couldn't stand, despite its beauty. I mean, even if I liked the Bay Area, there wasn't a naval air station up here. And I'd already planned to take a one-year unaccompanied tour to Okinawa, Japan next year.

Fuck, why was I thinking so far ahead? I hadn't even fucked this chick yet. Even worse, I hadn't even tried to sleep with her.

I called Beck.

As usual, he answered on the first ring. "Hey man, what's up?"

"Just dropped Sol off at her house." I paused. Beck usually didn't tolerate my locker room talk, but I needed to tell him about my night. "And get this. I didn't even try to sleep with her. What's wrong with me?"

Beck laughed. That cocky motherfucker. "Nothing's wrong with you—you just like her."

"I do. She's cool and smart. Cultured—she goes to the opera and shit. She took me to the best Chinese restaurant in the city and then we went to see the Blue Moon on Mount Tam."

"Man, you're sprung, and you don't even know it yet."

Fuck. How did this happen to me? "Well, I kissed her. I'm taking her on a date tomorrow, gonna see how she hangs at a dive bar. But that's it. I'll never see her again. We'll be in Seattle by Monday."

"Good. I'm glad you had a nice time with a good woman. But Huck, if you like her and you can somehow con her into liking you too, it doesn't have to be over. You're a pilot —you *can* fly anywhere any time you want, remember?"

"Whatever, dude. I just want to have a good time with her while I'm here. I'm not looking for a girlfriend. And I definitely have zero desire to start a long-distance relationship. Even you and Paloma were together for twelve weeks before you left for our tour. Plus, she lived with you. This is nothing more than a weekend fling. It is what it is. Anyway, I'll be at the hangar at zero six hundred."

"Sounds good. Later."

I drove across the bridge back to my hotel. Alone.

How had I fucked this night up? She could've been here with me now, but I hadn't even tried.

Well, the weekend wasn't over yet. I had tomorrow night to make her mine.

Even if it was for one night only.

CHAPTER 12
SOL

After Sawyer left last night, I couldn't sleep. I was consumed by thoughts of him and our kisses. I'd replayed our entire interaction in my head. I'd even dreamed about him. I was so excited to see him today.

I woke early and drove to the base. After walking through the maze of vendors, I entered the press box and waited for the show to start. Excitement rippled through me. Just two days ago, I'd been in that plane. Sawyer had only given me a preview of what he could do. Now I would see what he was really capable of in the air.

The crowd was milling around the base. Little boys and girls with toy planes stood by the gates, waiting to see a glimpse of their idols. Older men with baseball caps that displayed their status as military veterans also gathered around, but my eyes were drawn to a bunch of pretty women in tight skirts and low-cut tank tops, giggling and drinking champagne in the corner of the adjacent VIP box.

The groupies.

A burning sensation settled in the pit of my stomach. Seeing these women showed me the temptation Sawyer must face. But I didn't hold any ill will toward these women at all. I got it. Hell, I wanted to sleep with Sawyer. He was gorgeous.

I poured myself a glass of wine, adjusted my wide-brimmed hat, and posted a story.

"Hi, lovelies! Today I'm here at the air show where we'll actually see Sawyer and the rest of his squadron fly. I can't wait."

The announcer's voice rang out. "Ladies and gentlemen, please welcome your Blue Angel pilots!"

Sawyer walked out with the five other pilots in their tight flight suits and matching aviator sunglasses. They stood side by side with their arms behind their backs and then all of them took a wide stance in perfect unison. God, they were so hot standing together. They really did look like rock stars. They began walking in formation, never missing a beat. After they saluted the members of their aircrew, they each walked over to their planes.

The announcer introduced the first plane and then it was Sawyer's turn. "And flying Blue Angel number two from Davenport, Iowa, the right wing and the Marine Corps representative of the delta formation Captain Sawyer Roberts."

"Woo!!!!!" I yelled. The announcer's enthusiasm was infectious, and I beamed with pride that I knew Sawyer. That, better yet, I'd kissed him. Twice.

After introducing the rest of the pilots, the announcer spoke again. "The Blue Angel pilots take pride in personifying the United States Navy and Marine Corps values of honor, courage, and commitment."

Those words stopped me cold. *Honor, courage, commitment.*

Sawyer definitely had the courage to fly that plane and serve in the Marines Corps. He had committed to his company and squadron. I couldn't help but wonder if he could ever commit himself to one woman. Preferably me.

"The Blue Angels are the oldest performing United States military aviation demonstration team. Since 1946, they have exposed all generations to the wonders of naval aviation. And now, gaze up in the sky as our blues take to the air."

I screamed at the top of my lungs like a groupie. Mötley Crüe's song "Kickstart My Heart" blared from the speakers. I was so wrapped up in this moment watching Sawyer soar overhead, that I completely forgot I was supposed to be recording the whole thing.

Oh crap.

I pointed my phone toward the sky, but then something caused me to put the phone back in my pocket. My assignment was to post about the Blue Angels. There would be plenty of videos of the actual show and their death-defying formations. Plus, I was still going on a date with Sawyer tonight where I could post more pictures and maybe get a personal story about him.

But for now, for once in my life, I didn't want to watch through the lens of my phone. I wanted to experience the show with my own two eyes.

I stood on top of my chair, eager to see Sawyer's plane.

The first pass was a diamond formation with his plane just inches from the other three. Terror gripped me as they approached each other. He could crash. It was so dangerous. I actually didn't even blame the protesters for worrying that these Angels could collide and kill civilians on the ground now that I saw this performance firsthand. In my research, I'd read it had even happened before at another air show. I couldn't even imagine watching them crash live.

But they didn't crash—they flew perfectly overhead. It was surreal. How many hours had they practiced to make it look so effortless? And now that I had been in that plane, I knew there was more to flying than just skill. Sawyer and these men had to stay calm under pressure and maintain a laser-like focus so they wouldn't pass out. They had to avoid colliding with the other pilots, or even worse, crashing into the crowds below. One wrong move would mean death.

But Sawyer made it look like he was driving a car.

The music changed to "Dreams" by Van Halen. I was elated from the combination of the kickass DJ, the perfect day, and the excitement of seeing the planes. This was the best time I'd had in a while.

Even though I was standing here alone.

At least I wasn't watching it from my balcony.

Or on replay on my phone.

I was actually here participating. Living instead of observing.

The other day, I'd been so mad at Sawyer for giving me a hard time about my work, but now, I saw how important it was to be present in my life.

Now, four of the planes, including Sawyer's, were attempting to come from one side while the remaining two were approaching from the other side. I wanted to close my eyes—I couldn't possibly watch this—they were going to collide.

But they didn't.

The crowd roared, and desire built in me. I'd just gone from a small crush to a full-on obsession.

Oh my god! I was now a Blue Angel groupie.

Except, I wasn't a real groupie. I only wanted Sawyer, not the other Angels. And I hadn't even slept with him.

Then, a crazy idea occurred to me.

What if . . . I lost my virginity to him? Tonight.

Maybe I was just high from the excitement of the air show, but this sounded like an excellent idea.

I mean, why not? I was twenty-two years old. I was *so* sick of being a virgin. I'd never expected to still be a virgin at my age, and honestly, it made me feel like a freak. Sawyer had been so calm and soothing with me in the plane, so I was willing to bet he'd be an incredibly patient and experienced lover. And I was certain he was attracted to me. Hell, he had kissed me twice and was constantly telling me how beautiful I was.

Yes! This was a great idea. A one-flight stand with a Blue Angel. My first time would be with an American hero. A fighter pilot. My own TOPGUN. It would be like a fantasy come true.

But how would I make this happen? For some reason, men never openly propositioned me for sex or asked me to go home with them at bars, even though my friends never had this problem. And Sawyer hadn't even asked to come in last night. Even worse, I'd invited him in, and he had turned me down.

Clearly, I was the issue. Did I give off a prudish vibe? Maybe everyone could tell I was a virgin. Inwardly I shook my head—no, there was no way they could tell. I was just imagining the worst.

I needed to relax. Throw caution to the wind. Make it clear that I wanted him.

They flew for a bit longer, and my neck ached from straining to see them.

Finally, they landed. After exiting their planes, they walked over to the boxes, where their fans awaited.

And their groupies.

My nerve endings tingled when he headed in the direction of where I was standing, though there were hundreds of people here. Would he acknowledge me in the crowd? Assuming he'd even be able to pick me out of all the people gathered here.

There was yellow tape separating the fans from the pilots. Good idea. Someone could jump them. Someone like me.

I waved like a fool, and Sawyer winked at me. Yes, he acknowledged me. I felt like a million bucks.

He finally walked closer toward me, but a little boy with a stuffed toy in the shape of a Blue Angel plane jumped up toward Sawyer.

Sawyer knelt next to the little boy. "Hey buddy, did you like the show?"

"Yes. Can I be a pilot like you?"

"You bet you can. You just have to work hard in school, listen to your mama, and you'll be here one day." Sawyer hugged the little boy and the kid's mom, too. He then posed for a picture.

My breath hitched.

Then some other lady handed Sawyer her baby.

A baby!

Sawyer was cooing with the baby, a complete natural, and I was now dead.

I swear I felt sharp pangs in my ovaries. This was too much emotional overload for me.

By the time Sawyer finally reached me, my hands were shaking. Though he had kissed me last night, suddenly everything felt different. After seeing him fly, I felt so unworthy of his attention. Maybe he would ignore me or cancel our date.

His gaze focused on me. "What did you think, babe?" He flashed me a radiant smile, and I couldn't help returning it.

"I think . . . I think you're absolutely amazing. You've turned me into a Blue Angel groupie." I leaned into him and whispered into his ear, "I want to spend the night with you."

His eyebrow cocked, and he crossed over the yellow tape, leading me to a corner of the press box. He lowered his voice as he asked, "What are you doing, Sol? You're playing with fire."

"Maybe I want to get burned."

He crossed his arms. "Look, I don't know what you're doing teasing me like this. Listen to me—I'm a bad guy."

I shook my head. If only he could see himself the way I saw him—sweet on our date, kind to children at the show, comforting to me when we flew.

"No, you aren't, Sawyer. It's just an act. I see you."

"Babe, this can only ever be a one-night stand. Is that what you want, Sol? Just one night and I'll never see you again. I won't even be an Angel next year. I'll be stationed overseas."

Why was he resisting me so much? He probably thought I was just toying with him. I nodded my head. "Yes, it's what I want. I want you."

He cupped my face. "You don't strike me as the casual sex type."

Well, that was the understatement of the year. I'd never had any sex let alone casual sex.

"I'm not. But sometimes even good girls want to be bad."

A big smile graced his face. He led me back to the crowd, and then, right there, in front of the everyone, he pulled me tight against his chest and kissed me.

"You're mine tonight."

CHAPTER 13
SAWYER

The show was the best one yet of this tour. We'd been perfectly in sync. I thought the vibe would be ruined by the protesters, but even they didn't dampen our day. There was no feeling in the world like skimming the cables on the top of the Golden Gate Bridge with your five best friends.

But that wasn't even the best part of the air show.

It was seeing Sol cheering for me in the crowd after I landed. She squealed like a schoolgirl when she saw me. I'd never had anyone come to my shows with the sole purpose of being there to support me. Sometimes, I would watch the other pilots' wives standing there in the crowds, supporting their husbands, and I'd feel a pang of jealousy. I'd quickly wash away that emotion with some heavy liquor and some cheap sex. But sometimes, I wondered what it would be like to have someone cheering for my triumphs and worried for my safety.

Once I'd greeted Sol, she made my day even brighter by saying the words I'd longed to hear.

"I want to spend the night with you."

The second I finished with my air show obligations, we bounced. She hopped into my car, and we made out like teenagers at every stoplight. As she kissed me, her hand drifted closer to my cock.

I placed my hand at the top of her thigh, feeling the edge of her panties.

I was dying to sleep with her, but she was nothing like the women I usually hooked up with. Though she was aggressively pursuing me, and she seemed to be totally into me, something was *off* about her. I kept noticing that her hands were shaking, and she had a scared look on her face.

I pulled away from her.

"I don't get you, babe. You don't even like me."

She smiled. "Why do you say that? I definitely didn't like you at first, but you grew on me over time. Besides, who said I have to like you? I just want to have a good time.

One night. For once, not be the responsible one, the good one. I want to get wild."

God, what the fuck was wrong with me? She was giving me explicit consent, which I always required, but I still couldn't shake the feeling that she was hiding something.

Sol's lips were on fire. She grabbed my cock. "I want you to control me like you control your plane."

Fuck it. I'd turn off my mind and stop questioning everything. Still though, deep in my gut, I had a feeling something was wrong, and I'd learned to trust my intuition over the years. This gut had saved my life before and the lives of civilians, and it had never failed me. I'd find out what she was hiding once we were in my room.

Finally, we reached my hotel, and I parked.

We left the car, entered the hotel, and went to the elevators. I kissed her again, pressing her tight little body against the back of the elevator. Sure, we'd had a bit of a rocky start, but I couldn't believe I'd wasted two days with her not having sex. I should've fucked her the night of the gala, but in a way, I was glad I'd waited. Our last day together we would have sex. And by tomorrow morning, I'd be in Seattle. A perfect memory to end a perfect weekend.

Let's go out on a high note.

We reached the hotel room, and once we went through the door, I carried Sol to the bedroom. She kissed me back vigorously, passionately, like she couldn't get enough.

I'd had enough of this tease. I was going to fuck her all night.

I placed her on the bed and just stared at her for a moment. She was incredibly beautiful, and now she would be mine, if only for one day.

Her hair spread around her face like a halo, framing her gorgeous face. She was the angel; I was the devil. I kissed her neck, trailing down to her full breasts.

But when I looked back at her face, her lips were quivering. Was she cold? Or worse, scared?

Maybe she started having feelings for me and was upset I'd be leaving tomorrow. I hated to admit it, but I was beginning to have feelings for her, too.

Which was why I had to get away from her before I became addicted to her.

But she was here now. In my bed. I wanted to make sure she enjoyed herself. If she were nervous, I would reassure her.

"You okay, babe? We have all night. I'm in no rush—I can go slow."

She bit her lower lip and nodded.

Uh-oh. Something was definitely wrong. As much as I wanted to fuck her, I needed to see what was up.

"Sol, what's wrong? Do you not want to sleep with me? You don't have to."

She shook her head. "No. It's not that."

This girl was driving me crazy.

"Okay, so what is it? You look frozen. Or afraid. Did someone hurt you?" I pushed that thought out of my head because I couldn't even fathom some motherfucker abusing her. Even so, rage boiled inside of me. "Did some guy force himself on you?"

"No."

"Then what's wrong?"

"It's just that . . ." She trailed off and looked up toward the ceiling, then around the room. Anywhere, everywhere, but at me.

I cupped her face gently, forcing her to look at me. "Spill it, babe."

She exhaled so loudly I thought she was going to do the Hick maneuver.

Wait . . . I'd seen this hesitation before in other women. Usually, those ones were cheating on their partners. Once I found out, I'd kick them out of my room. I couldn't stand cheaters. Maybe Sol had a man. Hell, I'd be shocked if she didn't.

Jealously, a feeling that I had rarely experienced consumed me. Picturing another man fucking her made me want to punch something. "Do you have a boyfriend?"

She shook her head. "No, Sawyer! Why would you think that? If I had a boyfriend, I wouldn't be here with you like this right now." Part of me was relieved to hear she was unattached, but mostly I just wanted to know what was bothering her.

"Then what is it, babe? Just tell me."

She closed her eyes, then opened them slowly. "I'm . . . a virgin. I still want to have sex with you tonight, but I just thought you should know that I may not be that good. So, you have to go slow with me."

What the fuck . . .

A virgin.

My jaw literally dropped open. The thought had never occurred to me. And here I was about to sleep with her and never see her again.

What kind of monster was I?

I couldn't even formulate my thoughts. I had so many questions. But I just sat there like an idiot shaking my head in disbelief.

Finally, I said, "You're a virgin?"

Brilliant, Sawyer. She just told you that.

"Yup."

"How? I mean, you're beautiful. You're twenty-two. You've never had a serious boyfriend?" I knew her age from the bio on her resume. I had that thing fucking memorized. Just like I had the image of her beautiful heart-shaped face burned in my mind.

"I had one, but he was gay and eventually ended up coming out. And I mean, I've dated around but never too seriously. In high school, I was focused on getting into a good school and winning pageants. And after my boyfriend and I broke up at Stanford, between classes, charity work, growing my following, and pageant duties, I never had time to date. I guess I spend more time online than with people in real life."

This was precisely why I hated social media—all the connections were fake. What Sol and I had this weekend, our affection toward each other was all real.

"This isn't a religious thing?"

"No. I mean, I'm Catholic, but that's not the reason." She paused. "I didn't want to wait until I was married or anything like that. But I thought it would be nice to wait until I was in love and in a stable relationship."

Fuck! I needed a drink.

What the fuck was she doing with me in this hotel room?

I took her hand in mine. "Are you in love with me?" She burst into laughter, and I felt a little deflated, but at least I didn't have to worry she'd be hurt when I left tomorrow for Seattle.

"No, of course not. We've only known each other for a few days. I think you're gorgeous, and I haven't been able to stop thinking about you since we met. At first, I thought you were just a cocky jerk, but now I see that it's just façade you present to the world. You're a good man, Sawyer—kind, caring, sensitive. I liked the way you took care of me in the plane and after the flight. And the way you interacted with those kids at the show. I think I *could* fall in love with you if we spent more time together. But that'll never happen. You're leaving tomorrow, and I'm staying here. It is what it is. So, let's just enjoy the time we have left." She stroked my arm making my already hard cock throb.

I was dumbfounded. What was happening right now? What did she see in me that I didn't see in myself? Could I really become the man she thought I was? Did I even want to?

I closed my eyes and took a moment.

The shocking answer was yes.

For the first time in my life, I didn't want to run away from a woman. Usually, one-night stands were full of awkwardness and regret. I saw the sad looks on these women's faces when they asked when I would be in town next. When I would answer, "Not for a year or two," I would always get a reluctant nod. I didn't want to break anyone's heart, but my life was what it was.

I wanted to be the man Sol thought I was, though I doubted that she was right. Maybe I was just an arrogant motherfucker who could never get close to a woman and would always push her away. But maybe, just maybe, I was how she saw me—a decent man.

I wanted to try for her.

She gripped my thigh. "I still want to sleep with you tonight. Honestly, I've wanted that since we met, but I decided for sure earlier today. I'm ready."

But I'm not. God help me. I was about to turn down sex for the first time in my life. The even bigger irony was that I had never wanted to have sex with anyone more than I wanted to sleep with Sol.

I kissed her softly, enjoying the simplicity of this kiss. But then I took her hands in mine and sat down in front of her.

"I'm not going to sleep with you tonight."

She blinked back tears.

"Hey, don't cry, babe. It's not that I don't want to, because believe me, I do. I want to so badly. In fact, I've never wanted to have sex with anyone more than I want to have sex with you."

Her face widened into a smile. "Then, come on." She straddled me on the bed and wrapped her hand around the back of my neck, sending chills down my spine. She kissed me again and pressed her pussy against my cock.

"What's stopping you? I want you; you want me. I won't regret it."

I wanted to throw her down on the bed and make love to her all night long. Fuck her so hard that she'd be mine forever. Make her come. Knowing that she had only ever been with me would be the best gift I could ever have.

If I could be worthy of her love, maybe I could love myself.

"Yes, you will. You'll regret it tomorrow. And if not tomorrow, you will regret it two weeks from now or two months from now. You just told me you wanted to wait until you were in love and in a stable relationship with someone. That makes perfect sense. I think you should do that."

She pursed her lips and nodded her head really fast as if she was going to cry. "I understand. You're right. It's probably for the best. I wanted you to be my first, though. I'm crazy about you."

Don't worry, honey. I'll be your first, just not yet.

"Oh, babe, I'm going to take your virginity. I'm not going to let another man touch you. But not until you tell me you love me."

Her eyes opened wide, and I stared at her long, dark lashes. Could this woman really be mine?

"What are you talking about? You said that you don't have relationships. Ever. Plus, you're leaving for Seattle tomorrow, and I'm staying here."

"Yup, I'm going to Seattle, but you're coming with me." I exhaled. I couldn't believe I was actually going to ask her this. "Will you be my girlfriend, Sol?"

Her gaze narrowed. "You're messing with me. What are you talking about? I can't go with you. My life is here."

I laughed. "Not to be a dick, but what life? You said you have no friends, your family is traveling, and the person you talk to most is your PR agent. You spend your day in your condo posting Instagram shots." Her face fell as my harsh words hit her. I took her hand. "Follow me on the tour. You can post pictures from all the landmarks. Hell, I'll even take the damn pictures if you agree to be mine."

I couldn't believe I'd had just said that—I was about to become a fucking Instagram boyfriend. I used to mock those men I'd seen taking hundreds of shots of their girlfriends. But now, I understood them—they just wanted to make their women happy.

Like I wanted to make Sol happy.

A big smile graced her gorgeous face. She tackled me on the bed and kissed me. Joy rippled through me, just like how I'd felt the night Beck had called me to say, "Welcome to the squad, asshole."

"Yes! Oh my gosh, Sawyer, I'd love to." She kissed me and jumped into my lap. "I have so much to do. I have to get home and pack. And book my flight. Oh, I can do that now."

She tried to grab her phone, but I pulled her back into my arms. "Babe, you're flying with me."

"Fine, but no more tricks. I don't want to puke again."

"Deal. Instead, I'll show you some tricks now. I'm not done with you tonight."

I cupped her face with my hands and kissed her, my girlfriend, on her lips. The pressure in my balls built up and I was dying to fuck her or at least have her suck my cock. But I remembered how long I'd waited during tryouts for the Angels and reminded myself to be patient. Good things come to those who wait. And I was willing to wait for this beautiful woman to fall in love with me.

CHAPTER 14
SOL

Sawyer and I spent the night together, but we didn't have sex. I couldn't believe he had actually turned me down, especially since I could tell how much he wanted me, not to mention how hard he'd been when I'd practically thrown myself at him. But everything was different now. He had asked me to be his girlfriend. I wanted to scream it from the rooftop.

Or better yet, announce it on Instagram.

But I couldn't do that. I didn't want to piss him off. I knew how he felt about social media, and I wouldn't disrespect him.

It was *so* hard for me to live offline though. If you date someone and don't post about it on social media, does the relationship really exist? The answer, surprisingly, was yes.

I packed up some clothes and tidied up my condo so I wouldn't be embarrassed when the house sitter arrived, then I picked up the phone and called Kelli. She answered on the first ring.

"Hey, Sol. What's up?"

"Hey! I just wanted to give you a heads-up that I'm heading to Seattle for a few days."

Kelli laughed. "Are you serious? You wouldn't happen to be going with a handsome, daredevil pilot by any chance, would you?"

Ugh. I did not want to lie to her. But I also didn't know if I could trust her to keep the details of my love life to herself. She had access to my Instagram account, after all. She could post whatever and whenever she wanted. I didn't want to do anything to risk my fledgling relationship.

"It's just a weird coincidence—I have a friend from college who lives up there. I need a change of scenery. I'll make sure to get some good pictures."

She paused. "Fine." The sudden change in her tone confirmed that she hadn't believed a word I'd just said.

"Please email me about which theme you want to use in Seattle. Coffee is always great. Or seafood. I can arrange to get your hotel comped. And I'll send over a list of restaurants so I can arrange posts. I'll also contact some touristy places. Feel free to send me any ideas you have on your end. We might have to accept whatever we get because this is so last minute."

Right. This was my job. I could never have a trip that didn't involve business. I regretted not just absconding into the night and ghosting her. "Sounds good. I'll let you know the details. I do want to eat at Etta's. Not sure about the hotel yet because I may stay with my friend." *Boyfriend*, I wanted to say, but the "boy" was silent for now.

"Oh, right. Your *friend* from college. Okay. I'll be waiting for your itinerary. Bye, Sol."

Ugh. She was so on to me. "Bye."

I stared at my phone's glowing home screen for a few seconds after the call disconnected. Damn, that was tougher than I'd thought. If I continued dating Sawyer, news of our relationship would get out eventually. But I'd deal with that later.

Sawyer was already on base so he could prepare for the trip to Seattle, so I took an Uber to meet him. He greeted me with a big kiss. I giggled and just stared at him. This was so surreal.

Officer Daly smirked. "Miss Sol. Nice to see you again. You must be some woman to tame Sawyer. You can call me Beck."

"Hi, Beck. Thanks. I'm excited to go to Seattle. I haven't been in years."

"It's beautiful there. My fiancée will be joining us, so maybe we can all get together for dinner?"

Wow, I was being embraced by Sawyer's friends already. "Oh, I'd love that. I know this great restaurant in Seattle." I'd be getting paid to eat there and post about it, but he didn't need the details.

Beck shook his head. "Oh, let's skip the restaurant. Paloma's an amazing cook. I know I probably sound biased since she's my fiancée, but I think she's the best. She makes everything from scratch. Since the pilots travel so much during the year, we try to have home-cooked food whenever we can. We're basically one big family."

That sounded amazing. I loved how close they all were. No wonder Sawyer didn't need social media followers—he had real-life friends. What a radical concept.

"I'm so excited. That sounds wonderful. Thank you for welcoming me."

"Sure thing." Beck kissed me on the cheek and walked away.

I turned to Sawyer. "Wow, he's so nice."

Sawyer laughed. "Who, Beck? Beck is *not* nice. He's an excellent pilot, a good man, and a great dad, but he's definitely not nice. He's a hardass."

"Dad? Oh, how old are his kids?"

"His daughter Sky is a year and a half. His wife, Catherine, passed away during childbirth. Paloma was Sky's nanny, so that's how they met. She and Beck just got engaged."

"How heartbreaking. But that's so wonderful that he found love again. And I can't wait to meet Paloma."

"She's great. She raised her sisters practically all by herself. Beck's going to adopt them."

I was blown away. What an amazing story. I was excited to get to know Sawyer's friends and get a glimpse into the personal lives of these pilots.

Sawyer carried my luggage into the bay of the support plane that would follow us. I pondered riding with my bags for a second—at least I'd be guaranteed no stunts.

I stared at the massive blue jet on the runaway. Just looking at it made me ill.

I punched Sawyer's arm. "So, do you promise not to do any tricks in the air?"

He smirked and replied, "Yup, I promise. But you still have to wear a flight suit."

I pursed my lips. "Really? Why?"

He grinned. "Because you look smoking hot in it. The entire time you were flying with me, I was hoping your tits would pop out. Why do you think I did so many flips?"

"Oh my god! Really? I'm so embarrassed. And you're horrible."

He squeezed my ass then cupped my face. His lips took mine, and I melted into him. Our chemistry was explosive.

I knew he wouldn't sleep with me yet, but I couldn't wait to spend another night with him.

We boarded his plane. And this time, I wasn't scared.

The entire ride was smooth and calm. Sawyer honored my wishes and didn't do a single flip. I wanted to post a quick story about my private plane ride but decided against it. Social media detox was a struggle.

A few hours later, we finally touched down in Seattle. Light rain greeted us, but I didn't mind it. I was enchanted by the drizzle and grey, which was so different from the warm yet foggy weather back home. The chilly temperature built a strong desire in me to cuddle up with Sawyer, preferably by a crackling, roaring wood-burning fire.

Sawyer checked in at the new base while I called my college friend, Raine. She was the coolest girl, a professional ballerina with the Pacific Northwest Ballet. I thought I might get her voicemail, but she picked up right away.

"Sol? Hey, girl. What's up?"

"Hey, Raine. Totally random, but I just flew into Seattle."

"Really? That's awesome. We have to get together. I don't have a show going on now or anything, but I still have practice every day. Let's meet up for coffee soon, and you can take one of your pretty Instagram pictures."

Great. That was what I was known for—taking pretty pictures of coffee. Would that be my legacy? Was it really what I wanted for myself? Raine lived to dance, and Sawyer was so passionate about flying. What would make me truly happy?

"That sounds great. I'll have free time on most days. Text me the time and place, and I'll be there." I paused and then decided to tease her. "I have a secret to tell you, but only in person." I was dying to tell someone about Sawyer.

"Oh, I *love* secrets. Okay, I will text you for sure. See you soon. Bye."

"Bye."

Sawyer was still meeting with the crew, so I had some time on my hands. I perused some Seattle hashtags and began plotting my trip. I needed to email Kelli soon.

Normally, pictures of the local delicacies and sights filled me with excitement. I didn't know if I was feeling over-whelmed by my weekend with Sawyer, but for some reason, I didn't have any desire to work on this trip.

An hour later, Sawyer finally walked out of the administration office with keys in his hand. "We have the night off, and I have a rental car. Where would you like to go? I've been researching the best places for you to take pictures. We could head to Pike's Place Market or maybe the Space Needle?"

God, he was so wonderful! He was already thinking about what I wanted to do while I was here.

But he was dead wrong. I'd seen the most well-known sights of Seattle before. Spending time with Sawyer was the only thing on my mind right now.

"Actually, I just want to go back to the hotel room."

CHAPTER 15
SAWYER

Sol was already consuming my every waking thought. My mind battled my cock—I had been so resolute last night about not fucking her, despite her telling me she wanted to. She'd already said that she was ready to lose her virginity to me and there was no fucking way I'd let another man touch her, so why was I the one delaying the inevitable?

We checked into our hotel in downtown Seattle, right on the water. Normally, I'd have already been hitting up every hot spot in town, deciding where to eat and where to party later tonight. But now, I only wanted to spend my time with Sol.

The hotel clerk gave me the key to our suite. "Sir, the bellman will bring up your luggage."

No time for that. I planned to have Sol naked by then.

"I'll just grab the bags myself."

I winked at Sol, and she gave me a nervous smile. She had no idea what was in store for her.

Yesterday, I'd rushed her up to my hotel room, passionately kissing her in the elevator, desperate to fuck her.

But tonight, it was different.

I still wanted to fuck her, but that wasn't in the cards for us just yet. Instead, I wanted to worship her, explore her, taste her. And realistically, I knew that the first time we had sex would probably be painful for her. Until that moment came, I wanted her to only experience pleasure with me. I'd never slept with a virgin before, so I planned to do everything in my power to make sex live up to her romantic expectations. If she wanted candles, flowers, and chocolate-covered strawberries, I'd hook her up.

I opened the door to our room, and Sol's eyes lit up. She ran over to the balcony, which towered over a panorama of the entire waterfront.

"Oh wow! This suite is fabulous. Look at the view."

I smiled and nodded, but I was already staring at the most beautiful part of the view—the rich landscape was just the background.

"Do you want me to take a picture of you for your Instagram?"

She bit her lip. "No, it's okay. You don't have to."

This is her job, Sawyer. Respect it. "It's fine. I get it. I'm happy to do it if you need me to."

My girl lit up, and her lips widened into a dazzling smile. "Then I'd love one."

She briefly freshened up in the bathroom and then emerged, looking like a goddess.

She posed on the balcony, grinning and tossing her hair this way and that. After I took a bunch of pictures, she checked them all out, picked the best one to edit and posted it.

Then, I grabbed my own phone and pointed it toward her.

"My turn."

She pursed her lips. "Oh. Are you going to start an Instagram account?"

I shook my head. "Fuck no. I just want to take pictures of you." *So, when I'm overseas in hell or after you've left me once you find out what a prick I am, I can look at them and relive this moment.*

Fuck, I was turning into a total sap. Luckily, she couldn't read my mind.

She posed while I snapped photos. But I wanted more of her—not just pictures but for my memory.

I put down my phone. "Unbutton your blouse."

She licked her lips and didn't hesitate to undo her top button, giving me the tiniest glimpse of her cleavage. She was such a tease.

"I didn't tell you to stop. Keep going, babe."

She slowly undid all her buttons, all while maintaining eye contact. Her long hair cascaded down her chest, framing her gorgeous breasts. She was stripped down to a pretty purple lace bra that barely covered her nipples.

"Take off your jeans."

She turned around and pulled them off slowly, giving me a view of her perfect booty.

I walked over to her and spanked her ass playfully, and then turned her to face me.

She was utterly breathtaking. I loved her wide hips and thick thighs. My own beauty queen. I twisted my fingers through her black hair and pulled her into me. Normally, I didn't spend much time kissing, always just wanting to get to the main event. But not with Sol. I kissed her roughly and passionately, my tongue twirling against hers.

Our lips remained locked as I cupped her round ass. She leaned into me, and I could feel every inch of her luscious curves with only lace and lust separating me from her naked body.

I kissed around her face slowly, tracing every angle with my finger.

She kissed me back, pulled my shirt off, and unbuttoned my pants.

I expertly removed her bra and licked her left nipple as my thumb rubbed her right one until she moaned. Then I switched and sucked on her other nipple as her breathing began to quicken.

"Sawyer, that feels so good."

I lifted her up, and she wrapped her legs around my waist, rubbing her pussy on my cock. She tried to take my boxer briefs off, but I stopped her. I wanted to carry her into the bedroom and fuck her, but I held myself back.

Instead, I gently placed her down on the coffee table. I grabbed two pillows from the sofa and put one under her head and the other underneath her hips.

Her pupils widened, and her cheeks flushed.

I ran my fingers along the places where her panties met her skin and pressed my lips to her pussy over the fabric, inhaling her sweet scent.

Soaking wet. Fuck yes. I couldn't wait to taste her.

I kissed her soft belly and her thighs, enjoying the anticipation of seeing her let go. She arched her back as I pulled down her panties.

I'd been dying to see her pussy since I first met her.

It was as perfect as she was. A little triangle of neatly trimmed, curly dark hair. I blew a kiss on her soft lips.

I grasped her hips and pulled her ass to the edge of the table, hooking her legs over my shoulders and pressing my mouth against her pussy, taking a long, slow lick down the center.

She ran her hands through my hair. "Oh my god, Sawyer."

I wasn't sure what she liked—hell, I wasn't sure she even knew what she liked so I went slow—so slow it killed me. I explored her beautiful pussy, licking the folds, tasting her juices, rubbing her clit.

Her breathing became rapid, and her body tensed. I knew she loved it as she reached out and pulled my face against her pussy.

"That's it, baby. Go wild."

"Oh, yes!"

Her enthusiasm invigorated me. I licked her faster and slower, longer and shorter, deeper and shallower. I couldn't get enough. She tasted so sweet I drank her in.

Her hips bucked, and I was so turned on watching her. My cock throbbed, dying for relief.

I licked faster but didn't push my fingers into her pussy, not wanted to pop her cherry until we made love. Man, I bet she was so fucking tight. I couldn't wait to fuck her.

But I wouldn't tonight.

I moved back up to her breasts and sucked on her nipples as I worked her clit.

Her breath came in rapid spurts. "Sawyer—I . . ."

"Come on, baby. Just let go."

My mouth went back to her beautiful pussy, and I devoured her, sucking on her clit, kissing her, worshipping her. The more pressure I put on her, the more she moaned. And then, she started to writhe and gasp.

I didn't stop. I was determined in my mission.

I sucked on her clit. She let out a loud moan, and her body bucked as she came all over my face. I gave her a few minutes to catch her breath.

"Oh my God, Sawyer. That was amazing."

I pulled her up to me, brushed the hair back from her face, and kissed her forehead.

Mission accomplished.

CHAPTER 16
SOL

Last night with Sawyer had been incredible. I'd never come with a man before. Now I couldn't stop imagining how good sex would feel with him. I couldn't wait, but deep down, I was still afraid. Afraid I'd fall in love with him, lose my virginity to him, and then, he would leave me. Sawyer had been right—I was now positive that if I'd lost my virginity to him in San Francisco and had never seen him again, I would've been devastated and eventually regretted it. Not just for emotional reasons, either. I was already so addicted to how he made me feel that I'd be crushed if I couldn't sleep with him every night.

The next morning, Sawyer woke at five to head to the base to begin practicing for the air show, which meant I was on my own. I was a little sad that I wouldn't be spending the day with him but was going to make the best of the situation. I took a long, luxurious bath, scheduled a massage for the afternoon, and ordered room service.

I texted Raine, and luckily, she was available to meet me for coffee. I started to get ready when my phone rang.

It was Kelli.

"Hey. Don't worry. I'll be posting some more pictures later today."

"Great, Sol, but that's not why I'm calling. I just received an exciting opportunity for you."

"Really? In Seattle?"

"No. It's in Miami. Not this weekend but next."

Miami? An ache settled in my stomach. I wasn't interested. Not now. The next stop on the air show tour was in Pensacola, where Sawyer actually lived. I wanted to spend time with him in his home.

But Miami was close to Pensacola. So maybe we could go there for a day for the shoot. I could ask him . . .

But work wasn't a priority for me at this moment. For once, I was going to put my happiness first.

"I'm not really interested in accepting any new travel gigs right now. I have some money saved up, so I want to take a break and only go where I want to go. Focus on more authentic connections."

"Hilarious, Sol. You can take a vacation after this gig. Now's the time to strike while your engagement is hot. Your Blue Angels posts did incredibly well. It would be great if you could somehow post some more of those."

She was so on to me. My first thought was to confess to her that I was dating Sawyer and then post some pictures of him so I could keep my engagement high without having to accept a new job. But I kept my mouth shut —for now.

I ignored her leading statement. "So, what's the job?"

"This fashion mogul has requested that you take pictures at various locations in Miami. He's already sent a contract, and I've spoken to him. It's a wonderful opportunity for you. It's for one weekend, and it pays fifteen thousand dollars."

Whoa. Fifteen thousand dollars was nothing to scoff at. And the client had already sent a contract. I'd be a fool to let an opportunity like this pass me by all because I wanted to follow Sawyer around the country like some sort of lovesick puppy. I couldn't seem to focus on anything but him. Sawyer dominated my mind. I was so pathetic.

Maybe accepting this job would be a good opportunity to see if Sawyer and I had a fighting chance. If I could go away for a weekend and come back, and we still wanted to take this further, then maybe we could make this relationship work in the long run.

"And the guy's legit?"

"Yup, he checks out."

Granted, she thought that last guy was legit too, but that was a fluke.

"Okay, I'll consider it. Send me the contract, and I'll look it over."

"Sounds good. I'll email it now. I'd like to get this finalized by the end of the business day."

Well, no way that was going to happen—I needed to talk to Sawyer first. I wasn't going to blindside him.

"I'll try my best, but I can't guarantee I'll make a decision by tonight. I'm on the way to meet my friend today, so I'll be busy."

Kelli sighed. "Fine. I'll check in with you later today. Bye."

"Bye."

So much for my relaxing vacation in Seattle. I'd wait until I could go over the contract, talk to Sawyer, and then I would make a decision.

I finished getting ready, left the hotel, and walked down the street to meet Raine. I found the coffeehouse and immediately noticed her—somehow, she looked even more stunning than she had the last time I'd seen her. Her beauty was so natural and effortless, no stylist required. I was super envious. She wore a gray knit beanie on top of her cascading blonde locks, a thin lavender wrap sweater, and form-fitting black pants that showed off her slender frame. I wished I had her style, her confidence, and more importantly, her passion.

She embraced me and kissed me on the cheek. "Hi, Sol. You look great. You're practically glowing. This wouldn't have anything to do with your secret, would it?"

I gave a coy smile. "Maybe. You look fabulous as always. I love your cap. Let's get some coffee."

I perused the menu and ordered the ominously named Dark Side Roast.

I took an Instagram video of the barista making the incredible latte art in the shape of Darth Vader. My fans would love this picture. After posting and hashtagging, I grabbed my drink and sat down next to Raine. I took a sip of the coffee; it tasted even better than it looked.

Raine was smiling at the hot barista, who was totally checking her out. She just dripped sex appeal. I gave her a nudge and said, "Earth to Raine! Don't you want to hear what's going on with me?"

She smirked at me knowingly. "Okay, tell me your secret."

Nerves got the best of me. "In a bit. First, tell me what's new with you? What ballet are you in?"

"Nope. Not telling you anything until you spill the tea— or the coffee, in your case. Are you dating someone? That hot pilot you posted on your Instagram? Please tell me you finally got laid."

I could feel warmth flood my cheeks. My virginity was an open secret among my friends.

I shook my head. "No. We haven't had sex, not yet anyway. But yes, I'm dating that pilot. His name is Sawyer, and I'm obsessed with him." My heart raced when I thought of him. Captain Sawyer "Huck" Roberts. Even his name filled me with joy.

"I knew it! Woman, I saw the video of you flying in his plane. You're insane but very brave. I would never ever go up in that jet no matter how hot the guy was. And he's gorgeous."

"Brave? What a joke—I was scared to death, but he was so patient with me. And he is hot, isn't he? You should see his body."

"Then *why* haven't you slept with him? Have I not taught you anything? You're not still dreaming of finding true fairy-tale love, are you? That only happens in the ballet, and even in the best ones, one of the lovers ends up dead. Just have some fun."

I laughed. "I want to, and in fact, we were about to, but I ruined the moment by telling him I'm a virgin. He was super shocked. I think it totally threw him for a loop. So, we talked, and he decided that it would be best if we waited until we were more serious. I mean, we only met four days ago."

Raine rolled her eyes. "Sol, you're beautiful. He turned you down? Is he gay like Ben? You wasted two years on that guy with his 'I want to wait for marriage' bullshit. You totally fell for it. I *told* you he was gay, and you refused to believe me. I have the best gaydar—I'm a professional dancer, for fuck's sake."

Ah, Ben. He had been the best boyfriend, but I'd been so blind to his lack of attraction to me. In public, he'd be all over me, but in private he wouldn't touch me with a ten-foot pole. I didn't blame him—his parents were ultra-religious and literally tried to convert him when he finally came out to them. Even now they still hadn't come around and had actually disowned him. Ben and I were still friends, and I'd care about him forever, but I had to admit, the years of feeling undesired had definitely taken their toll.

"No, Raine. Sawyer's not gay. Like at all. If anything, he's a player. After the plane ride, he asked me out to a gala, but we totally clashed. He was annoyed by me posting on Instagram, and he was rude and condescending."

"What a jerk. Then why are you here with him?"

"Well, he apologized. He bought me flowers, and we started all over."

"And?"

"And, I don't know, we spent the whole weekend together. We had our first kiss on Mount Tam under the moonlight during the Blue Moon."

"Oh, that sounds romantic."

"It was. And he was *so* sweet. And once I saw him fly, I was hooked. I mean, everyone treats him like a god. And he was talking to these kids after the show, and he even held a baby. I was so turned on by the whole thing. So, I decided I wanted to lose my virginity to him."

"But he turned you down."

I pursed my lips, a little embarrassed. "Yeah, he did, but nicely. I don't know, like when I told him, he was visibly moved. I can't explain it. I saw a full shift in him. And then, he asked me to come to Seattle with him. And to be his girlfriend. We've fooled around, which was incredible. I couldn't believe how amazing he made me feel. Well, *he's* amazing. I'm thrilled, so I just hope it works out."

She reached across the table and squeezed my hand. "I'm happy for you, Sol. I mean it. You deserve all the best things in life. But you shouldn't place so much stock in your virginity. If you want to sleep with him, sleep with him. If you don't want to sleep with him, don't sleep with him. Sex is great when you're comfortable with your body —I've learned that by being a dancer. But it doesn't guarantee that a relationship will work. Just enjoy yourself and whatever happens, happens. If you're meant to be together, it will work out. If not, you'll at least have had your first time with a gorgeous man who's probably an incredible lover."

I exhaled. Raine's words made so much sense. For years, losing my virginity had been such a big deal for me. But I was an adult, and I just wanted a normal, healthy relationship. Sex was a part of that. Raine had always had such a sex-positive outlook. Her mom was incredibly open and honest, and Raine had never been raised with any of the pressure that I'd had to save my virginity to give as a gift to my future husband. Raine would always fall for guys, have torrid love affairs with them, and then they would have no drama when they went their separate ways. Raine's true passion was dancing. She was so focused on her career that she never lost herself in a relationship.

I turned the tables on her. "Okay, secret told. So, what about you? How's the ballet? Do you like living in Seattle?"

"Things are great here, but I miss the sunshine, though my name is Raine so maybe I'm destined to live here. I just was promoted to soloist. I really wish you could see me dance while you're in town, but we don't have a show right now."

"Oh, that's great. Congratulations. Yeah, I'd love to come back next time you have a performance. Are you dating anyone?"

"No, nothing serious, but I have some friends with benefits. Or if I really want to get laid, I just find someone on Hinge. I'm just focusing on becoming a principal dancer. A man is not a priority. I definitely don't have time for a relationship."

Raine always impressed me—she knew exactly what she wanted. Why couldn't I be as self-assured as she was? Maybe she had the right attitude. Maybe I should sleep with Sawyer tonight simply because I wanted to. If it worked out, it would work out. If it didn't, I would have a beautiful memory. Maybe I shouldn't have followed him to Seattle. My mom used to tell me a man should chase me, not the other way around. I needed to be more like Raine. Find my true passion and embrace it. Not neglect my job for a man.

Finally, I had some clarity.

Raine and I chatted more before finally saying goodbye.

I checked my phone and saw the email from Kelli with the contract. I quickly read it.

Being photographed in some of the most exclusive spots in Miami was such an amazing opportunity. Kelli was right —the contract was solid. I didn't need to wait to ask Sawyer. I'd already made up my mind.

I picked up the phone and called Kelli.

"The assignment looks great. I'm in."

"Good girl, Sol. I knew you'd make the right choice. Okay, you leave next Friday."

"Next Friday?"

"Yup."

"Okay, I'll be there."

Friday. That meant I had less than two weeks left with Sawyer before I went. But that should be fine because I was sure he'd be busy with the air show this weekend.

I needed to tell him tonight.

CHAPTER 17
SAWYER

The second my plane touched down after practice, I grabbed my phone to text Sol. I was dying to kiss her again. I'd told her we should wait to have sex, but after last night, I didn't know how much longer I could resist her. Maybe I was overthinking things. Wasn't it enough that we were dating? If we slept together, it wouldn't be a one-night stand.

I gathered my gear and changed out of my flight suit into jeans and a T-shirt. My phone's notification light blinked, indicating I had a message.

Sol: I just got back to the hotel room. I'm going shower and can meet you wherever.

I didn't want to go to another Instagram-worthy place. Between getting ready for the gala and wearing a suit at the Chinese restaurant, I was over getting dressed up. I just wanted to grab a beer, shoot some pool, chow down on a burger, and hang out with Sol. I thought for a second about what to say to her.

Me: Cool. There's a great dive bar across the street from the hotel. I can pick you up.

Sol: Let me get ready. I'll just meet you there.

Me: Sounds good.

Awesome. I sent her a link to the place. Tonight, I wanted to see if she could kick it and just be real.

Declan stood in front of me. "Where you heading?"

"To the bar across from our hotel. Sol will be joining me later. Want to come?"

"Yeah, I'll hang out for a bit."

Cool. We drove to the hotel, left the car with the valet, and then walked across the street to the bar. I texted Sol to let her know we'd arrived. She texted back that she'd be joining us in a bit.

A thick haze of smoke and the scent of stale liquor and grease wafted over us as we entered. Yup, just my kind of place. A place to drink and unwind. To dissolve into the crowd. To blend in, not stand out.

Damn, Sol would hate it here.

Declan and I sat at the bar and ordered beers and burgers. The bartender poured our drafts, and I sank into the pleather stool.

Declan punched my arm. "So, what's happening, Romeo? I've never seen you so hung up on a chick."

I took a swig. "Yeah, I don't know. Sol's beautiful, no doubt, but we have nothing in common."

He laughed. "That's never mattered before. Remember Miss Cherry? That chick was a goddamn mess. What's different this time?"

Damn, Miss Cherry was a trip. But I didn't want to think about her, all I could think about was Sol.

I needed to tell Declan about how I felt about Sol. In all truth, I had no one else who really understood me. Beck was too judgy, too perfect.

"Sol's a virgin."

Declan spat out his beer. "Shut the fuck up."

"No, seriously. I was shocked, too. But she swears she is, and I believe her. And I know it shouldn't matter, but it does. She wanted to sleep with me, lose her virginity to me, and I told her no."

"*You* turned her down? You? Fuck-me Huck? Mr. Girl in Every City? Love them and leave them? See you next year? Don't call me, I'll call you? Are you feeling okay? Too many aerial loops gone to your head?"

Hearing Declan call me out on my bullshit rattled me. He was right. That was who I was, who I'd always been. But I had my reasons. Beck and Declan grew up in stable families and had loving parents. I'd told them both bits and pieces of my past, but I'd always omitted one dark secret. One I'd never share with anyone. Not Beck. Not Declan. And definitely not Sol.

Some secrets were meant to be taken to the grave.

"Yeah, me. And, I'm fine. Never better. She's beautiful and smart. Classy—I find her fascinating. And she stands up to me. Also, if she's been a virgin this long, I bet she'll stay faithful to me when I deploy. I know I just met her, but I've never felt like this about any woman."

Declan shook his head. "Well, you're a mess, but you've always known that. And not all women cheat—Beck's wife never cheated."

"Right. She didn't. Catherine was perfect. Then she died."

"Huck, that's not the point. Life is messy. People die. But they loved each other. If you asked Beck, he would tell you he didn't regret a second of loving her and would do it again, even knowing how it would end. And they had Sky together, so Catherine lives on through their daughter. Plus, now he's engaged to a wonderful woman who loves Sky like she's her own daughter. He never lost faith."

I hung on the word *faith*. That was where Declan and Beck had me. Faith. I didn't have any faith. Like at all. I wasn't religious. I didn't believe in anything.

"Well, for now, I'm just happy she came to Seattle with me. It can't last anyway—I already put in for unaccompanied orders to Okinawa next year. It is what it is."

Declan knocked back his drink. "We both know orders can be changed. Especially for an Angel."

"But that's the point, man. I don't want my orders changed. I just want to live my life. I want to live overseas. I want to travel without being tied down to a woman or putting down roots. I mean, Sol's great and all, but I really don't see this going far."

Declan nodded. Unlike Beck, he knew when to push me and when to back off.

The bartender served us our food. I could always count on Declan to come out with me to grab a greasy burger with some crisp fries. One bite soothed my soul. This was exactly what I needed—comfort, familiarity, satisfaction.

I checked my phone. Still no word from Sol. Where was she?

Declan opened his mouth like he was going to ask me another question. I didn't want to talk about my feelings anymore, so I spoke first.

"Are you excited to get back to Pensacola?"

"Definitely. My parents live there."

Parents. Good excuse, but I knew why he wanted to go home so badly. Declan was hoping to see his ex, but every time we went there, he never found her. An ex from ten years ago. I didn't understand why he couldn't forget her, but then again, I'd never been in love.

Would I feel the same way when Sol left me?

I guessed some people never moved on—glad I wasn't one of them.

"Be real, dude. You're just hoping to find your ex."

"Well, she moved away. No one's heard from her for years. But yeah, man, I do wish I could see her again. You don't get it. You've never been in love, so you don't know what it's like. The whole world melts away, and there's only you and her."

"Well, if it's so great, how did you fuck it up?"

"You're such a dick, man. I didn't fuck it up. She dumped me when I got into Annapolis. I would've stayed in Pensacola for her, but she made me promise to go."

"If you were so in love, why didn't you date long distance like Beck and Catherine had? Which, by the way, I think is a stupid idea. Out of sight, out of mind."

When I said those cruel words, Declan's face tightened. But maybe it wasn't that easy to forget someone. Since I had met Sol, I couldn't stop thinking about her. Maybe if I ever fell in love, I would think about my woman all the time also.

"I wanted to, but she didn't. She said it would be too hard for both of us, so she dumped me. And then she moved away. I don't even know where she is."

"That's brutal." I looked toward the door right as Sol sauntered in. I expected her to look out of place, but instead, she was wearing a skintight tank top with a black bra peeking out from underneath, tight jeans, and red high heels. It reminded of that scene in that movie *Grease* where Sandy turned into a bad girl for Danny.

Maybe Sol wanted to be bad.

I dashed over to her before one of the dickheads in this bar got his paws on her. I pulled her in for a kiss and squeezed her incredible ass.

"You look sexy as fuck."

"Thanks, babe."

Her eyes danced over the bar, and she tried her best to hide her disgust, but I could sense her discomfort. But to her credit, she didn't complain.

I walked her over to Declan, and she flashed him a bright smile.

"Hi, Declan."

"Hey, Sol. Sawyer's been talking about you nonstop."

She smiled, and I glared at Declan.

I put my hand on her hip from behind to get her attention. "What do you want to drink, babe?"

"I'll have a rum and coke."

At least she got the hint that there were no pretty picture-worthy drinks in here with glass rims dipped in crushed candy canes.

She turned to Declan. "Your show the other day was amazing. I'm so impressed."

"Thanks."

"Are you a Marine, too?"

"No, I'm in the Navy. Your boyfriend is the only Marine on the squad."

I wanted to kick him in the balls for his *boyfriend* comment, though it was accurate. The title just seemed foreign to me. And who knew how long we would last?

"You hungry, babe?"

She shook her head. "No thanks, I already ate." She paused and glanced at the bar seat, which was slashed; probably by a knife. "So why do you like this place?"

I smirked. She was cute when she was uncomfortable. "Because it's real. No pretense. Just hard liquor and real food. What you see is what you get."

She licked her bottom lip. "So, kind of like you?"

"Exactly like me." I wrapped my arms around her little waist and rested them on her wide hips. She wasn't even wearing much makeup. Her dark eyes glowed. Her fans might worship the face she presented to social media with all her filters, but I was certain she'd never looked so beautiful in her life than she did staring at me in this smoky bar.

"Is this the kind of place you hung out at back in Iowa?"

"Yup. I've never felt comfortable in nice places—even at the academy. I always felt judged."

She tilted her head and winced. "Did you feel like I was judging you at that restaurant?"

"No, of course not. But I just want to get to know you. The real you. Not Miss Solana San Francisco."

She laughed, and I noticed the freckles on her cheeks. I'd never seen them before. They must've been hidden under her makeup. "You think I can't hang out in a bar?"

"I don't know—prove it to me."

She signaled to the bartender and ordered a shot of tequila. When he delivered it, she downed it without hesitation.

"That's my girl. Let's go shoot some pool." I led her over to the lone pool table at the back of the bar.

"I'm going to put a song on."

She walked over to the jukebox nearby and flipped through the music selections.

She finally chose a song, and a few minutes later, "You've Lost That Loving Feeling" started playing.

Ha!

I grabbed her in my arms. "Do you like playing games, little girl?"

"Only with you. You promised to serenade me."

"I have to be in my uniform for that."

I pressed her back against the edge of the pool table and kissed her. I wanted to throw her down and take her then and there. How hot would that be?

Deep breath, Sawyer. I was in for a world of hurt tonight with no relief.

I released her and knocked back a drink, then racked the balls while she grabbed a cue stick. I laughed knowing that she also had my balls in the palm of her hands.

"I call stripes. Watch this." She bent over the table and broke, two balls dropping in each of the farthest corners.

Damn. "Ah, I get it now. You've been hustling me all along. So, are you some kind of pool shark?"

"No. But my dad had a table in his garage. My friends and I would always play. Are you up for a wager?"

Fuck yeah, I wanted to make a wager. My heart raced. She was so confident and sexy, comfortable in her own skin. And she had transformed from an uptight beauty queen into my perfect naughty girl, not just with her clothes, but also with her attitude.

"What do you want to bet?"

She wrapped her arms around my neck. "If I win, you'll make love to me tonight."

"Then I'll make sure to lose." I kissed her. "Babe, you don't need to make a bet with me for that. I'll fuck your brains out right now. I just thought you would want to wait."

"And I appreciate that. You were right, it would've been a mistake in San Francisco because you were about to leave, and I would've been crushed. But you are now my boyfriend, and I'm here with you now. I like you. We don't need to make promises for the future. I'm just happy to know that it won't be a one-night stand. And that you're open to seeing where this relationship goes."

I cupped her face in my hands and kissed her again. She was so wonderful. "Are you sure?"

"Yes. Positive. I just want you to make me feel as good as I felt last night."

"I can guarantee that. I'll make you feel even better, babe. Let's get out of here."

I put my arm around her, said goodbye to Declan who was still drinking at the bar, and had to fight the urge to throw Sol over my shoulder and sprint back to the hotel.

CHAPTER 18
SOL

"**B**abe, I'm crazy about you."

Sawyer shoved me against the side of the bar's exterior, the rough bricks scraping against my back. His lips attacked mine, and this kiss was different than any of the kisses I'd had before. He was rough yet sweet, and his hands gripped my thighs.

"Me too."

I was dying to feel him inside me. No more teasing. Based on how he made me feel last night, I was sure I was in for the best night of my life.

We crossed the street back to our hotel, dashed inside, made out in the elevator, and all but sprinted to our suite.

Sawyer opened the hotel door and then picked me up like a bride and carried me into the room. But our romantic moment came crashing down the second the bed came into focus.

There was a naked platinum-blond woman spread eagle on the bed with whipped cream and cherries over her breasts and bikini line.

What the fuck? I climbed out of Sawyer's arms. A sudden chill replaced the heat that had just been in my core.

Sawyer's eyes bulged.

"Veronica, what are you doing here? I told you I couldn't see you while I was in town."

Veronica? You know her name? I turned to face Sawyer, hoping for answers to my silent questions, but his blank stare gave me nothing, so I focused back on Veronica.

She pointed a perfectly manicured, electric purple fingernail at me. "Oh, so *she's* the reason you didn't want to see me? She doesn't look like your type, Huck. She doesn't even have a tramp stamp."

How did she know whether or not I had a lower back tattoo? I looked down at my tank top and saw it riding up my back. And I had briefly turned toward Sawyer. Ah, well, at least she was observant.

Veronica stood up, buck naked except for the whipped cream, and walked over to Sawyer. Wow, she had a great body. And clearly, she was wild in bed. I understood perfectly why Sawyer would rather sleep with a sex kitten than a chaste virgin. I should just run out of this room and leave them alone.

Sawyer's eyes blazed with fury. "How'd you get in my room?"

"I work here, remember? Don't worry. I'll leave."

Veronica went into the bathroom.

Sawyer turned me toward him. "Babe, I'm sorry. I didn't know—"

I looked straight into his eyes and did my best to keep my voice calm and steady. "We can talk when she leaves."

A few minutes later, Veronica emerged from the bathroom, dressed in a short jean skirt and a white tank top. She was effortlessly beautiful, and as much as I wanted to hate this woman for giving me a glimpse into Sawyer's past, I couldn't. I was in awe of her confidence.

She touched my hair, and I jerked away. "Sweetheart, enjoy this one while you can. He fucks like a rock star but has a girl in every city."

My throat burned. I wanted to draw myself a bath and cry in the tub.

Then, Veronica placed her hand on Sawyer's chest. He quickly moved it off of him and stepped back, which caused her to laugh. "Bye, Huck. Call me next year."

And then she walked out the door, shutting it behind her.

Once she was gone, Sawyer and I just stood there in silence.

Finally, he spoke. "Sol, I can explain."

I shook my head. "No, it's fine. You don't have to. I get it. She's your Seattle girl." My voice cracked. "Sorry I ruined your plans by tagging along. I can fly home. I'll get my own room tonight, and you can call her to come back. No need to wait until next year."

He shook his head. "Babe, stop. You're right—I don't have to tell you, but I want to tell you. Sol, please, listen."

I blinked back tears. To think that I was about to lose my virginity to this man, and he had a backup waiting in his room. I was such a fool. I just wanted to go home.

But then I looked at him again. And although I was the one who had just been humiliated, he was the one who looked broken. It wasn't like he'd cheated on me. I needed to hear him out.

"Fine, speak."

"Sol, I've never lied about who I am. I'm a womanizer. Like Veronica said, I have a woman in every city. When I come back to each city, sometimes I see the same woman again. I saw Veronica last year. She'd texted me the other night after I met you, and I told her that I didn't want to see her. But she came anyway. I really had no idea she would show up. I'm sorry. It was just sex. I never cared about her."

"I don't even know how you can say that. I mean, I hear you, but how could you not care about someone you sleep with?"

"I just don't. Sex is sex. It's relief, a good time, a high. It's never meant anything to me."

My throat tightened. I was disgusted by his words, but I appreciated his honesty.

But my pain provided clarity. "I want to apologize for continually leading you on. This was a wake-up call for me as well. I guess I don't have to be in love to have sex, but I really want it to mean something, not just to me, but to both of us."

He nodded then and walked over and hugged me. I accepted his embrace and felt comforted by him despite my anguish. What was I doing with him? Could a man really change? Someone who was that much of a womanizer couldn't possibly be faithful to one woman, could he? And Veronica seemed uninhibited—I doubted he could ever be satisfied by an innocent virgin like me.

"Sol, it *would* mean something. I've never known anyone like you. Any other woman would be flipping out right now. You aren't yelling at me or blaming me. I don't deserve you."

I led him over to the bed and sat down next to him. We needed to talk.

"I'm not mad at you. Or hurt even. You didn't betray me. We only met a week ago. You've been nothing but respectful and patient with me. But I need to be honest, too. I think the way you view sex and intimacy is sad. I know I don't have a clue what I'm talking about because I'm a virgin, but I really think you should genuinely care about the person you have sex with. It just has to make it better."

He stroked my cheek and gave me a sweet kiss on my lips. "That sounds great, but my lifestyle makes it hard to have a serious relationship."

I rolled my eyes. "That's not true. Your friend Beck has had two committed relationships. You choose to have meaningless sex. Why?"

"Because it feels good."

I was getting nowhere. "Well, I'm not equipped to diagnose you, but I can tell you one thing for sure—your attitude about sex isn't healthy. Can I ask you a question?"

He exhaled. "Shoot."

"Tell me about your past."

He moved a bit farther away from me. He did not like talking about himself.

"Nothing to tell. My mom was a single mom; I didn't see her much. Don't even know who my father is. My mom left me alone and with random people all the time. I saw *Top Gun* as a kid and wanted to be a pilot, so I studied hard in school and got into the Naval Academy."

"And?"

He tilted his head and swallowed hard. "And that's it. I graduated top of my class, joined the Marine Corps and then went to fighter school."

He was so detached; his words filled me with sadness. More importantly, he was holding something back from me, but I wasn't going to push. "Do you still see your mom?"

"No, and I don't care to. She wasn't there for me, so I don't feel the need to be there for her."

"And that's it? Have you ever had a serious girlfriend?"

"No. Sometimes, I've seen girls more than once, but I've never been in a relationship. I don't want to be responsible for anyone else but myself."

My turn to exhale. *Because you don't know how to love or be loved.* Those psychology classes I'd taken toward my degree were really coming in handy. My heart broke for him.

"What do you want from me? Why did you invite me to Seattle? Tell me the truth, Sawyer. Was it just because I'm a challenge? A virgin?"

He shook his head. "No. It wasn't just that. I like you, Sol, I really do. You're beautiful, of course, but you're also so sweet and kind. And I like that you stand up to me. I don't really know what I'm doing or where this can go, but I like being around you. This is going to sound cheesy as fuck, but I want to try to be the man you think I am."

A smile returned to my face. "You are that man. I believe in you. I care about you."

He pulled me to him and pressed his body against mine. Our lips met, and I got lost in our kisses. If Sawyer could actually enjoy our innocent intimacy that didn't involve sex, maybe he could genuinely emotionally connect with me. Though I was a virgin, it was quite possible I knew more about love than Sawyer did.

CHAPTER 19
SAWYER

I was so grateful Sol hadn't left me after that stunt Veronica pulled. I couldn't believe she'd entered my room. Sure, we'd had a good time last year, but I had told her I couldn't see her when I was in town this time. She had texted me to say she was sorry, and I had told her no worries.

But in a strange way, the whipped cream incident had brought Sol and me closer together. We were still slowly getting to know each other, and with sex off the table, we were spending our time together in places other than bed. And I hated to admit it, but who knew what would've happened if we'd slept together the other night. I might've panicked and ghosted her, which would be unforgivable because I actually liked her. So, for now, we were taking it slow. So slow that my balls were in a world of hurt.

Sol emerged from the bathroom dressed in a floppy hat and a bright turquoise sundress that ended right on her juicy thighs. I wanted to devour her. "Ready?"

"As ready as I'll ever be." As part of my punishment, I had agreed to accompany Sol around the city to take Insta-grammable photos. To me, I thought that meant typical tourist destinations like Pike Place Market or the Space Needle, but Sol wanted something unique. So, we were headed to visit some murals around town.

I grabbed her duffel bag, which was filled with different clothing options, and we headed out.

We arrived at the first place and met her photographer, Joy. Luckily, Sol didn't expect me to take the photos myself. I was sure I would've fucked that up. She'd hired a local photographer who'd brought a camera and lighting and all the equipment Sol would need. I was just there for support.

Sol introduced me to Joy.

"Nice to meet you, Sawyer. Will you be in any of the pictures with Sol?"

Sol laughed nervously. "Oh no. The pictures will just be of me."

I forced a smile. I appreciated that Sol wasn't asking me to be in the photos with her. I guess it was a source of contention between us since I'd made a big deal out of her doing that story on us when I'd picked her up for our first date at her place in Sausalito. She'd gone out of her way during this entire week in Seattle not to include me in her daily stories. Even so, I wasn't embarrassed to be seen with her. Quite the opposite—I liked showing her off.

A few hours later, we were at Pier 66. I was antsy and starving. I just wanted to steal Sol away and take her somewhere local, like to the Mukilteo Ferry to get a delicious cup of clam chowder.

Sol ran over to me and gave me a kiss on my cheek. "Sorry, babe. You've been amazing. I'll make it up to you."

I pulled her into my arms and kissed her. The world melted away as I became drunk on her taste, but I was bumped back into reality when a bright flash went off.

Joy had the camera pointed right at us. "Sorry! You just both looked so adorable with the Ferris wheel in the background. I couldn't resist."

Sol bit her lip. "Don't worry. I won't post that picture. I'll just keep it for us. For memories."

I walked over to Joy. "Let me see the picture."

She showed me the display on her camera. The shot was beautiful. Sol's long hair was cascading down her shoulders, and my arm was placed around the small of her back. Her left foot was lifted off the ground.

She looked stunning. We looked like we were in love.

Were we?

No, definitely not in love. We'd only known each other for a week. Even so, my feelings for her were growing stronger every day.

A protective desire grew inside me. I wanted not only to show Sol off to the world but also to claim her as mine. I had to admit I was sick to death of the constant DMs her lovesick admirers always sent her. If Sol received one more dick pic, I'd lose it.

I grabbed Sol's hand. "You look gorgeous in that picture. You should post it."

Her forehead creased as she looked at it. "Are you sure? I mean, it is a great picture. My followers will love it. But they'll start asking questions."

I kissed her again. "Let them. In fact, just tell them I'm your man."

CHAPTER 20
SOL

I grabbed my phone and checked my Instagram after I posted that picture with Sawyer. I was drowning in DMs.

OMG Sol! Is that the pilot?!

Uh yeah . . . didn't she see the plane and the pilot emojis?

He's so hot! Is he your new boyfriend?

Damn straight. I almost died when Sawyer agreed to let me post the picture of us and when he told me to tell my followers he was my man. I wanted to scream with joy, but that would've been so over the top. So, I did a simple post: *Dreamy day with my man.* And sure enough, everyone freaked out.

Including Kelli.

She'd been thrilled, of course, but wanted me to include him in regular pictures. She also made me promise that I wasn't going to flake on going to Miami.

Miami.

I hadn't even told Sawyer about it. I didn't know what to say. I mean, this was my job, so I was sure he would understand. But for some reason, I was incredibly anxious about telling him I was going away for the weekend. And after I saw Veronica in our room, I was paranoid about leaving him, especially in his home base of Pensacola where I was sure he had a ton of women on speed dial. Would he cheat on me? Especially since we weren't having sex yet?

I needed to give him the benefit of the doubt. We couldn't build a relationship if I was constantly suspicious. He hadn't done anything to disrespect me yet. We just needed more time to get to know one another and understand each other's worlds.

Tonight would help me on that front. Beck's fiancée Paloma was cooking dinner for the entire squad.

I nervously put on my makeup and curled my hair. After settling on a colorful blouse with white pants and heels, I got dressed and walked over to Sawyer, who was watching television on the sofa.

He looked at me and kissed me. Everything seemed so normal between us. Like we'd been together for years.

"Let's go."

We drove into Kirkland, where Beck and Paloma were staying at an Airbnb.

Beck greeted Sawyer and then gave me a kiss on the cheek. "Sol! I'm pleasantly surprised to see you again."

Sawyer ignored him. I didn't understand their relationship. I wasn't sure if it was playful ribbing or veiled disgust. Either way, it was clear that Beck doubted Sawyer could be in any sort of a relationship. I wasn't sure what to make of that, so I tried to focus on making a good impression.

"Nice to see you, too. I hope to be around for a while." Sawyer gave Beck a smug smile.

"I hope you are, too. This is my lovely fiancée Paloma and our little girl Sky."

I stared at Paloma, who was drop-dead gorgeous. She was cradling blond-haired, blue-eyed Sky. I adored how Beck referred to Sky was "our little girl." He clearly had no problems maintaining a relationship while being a Blue Angel, which proved Sawyer's excuse that it was impossible was all in his head.

"Nice to meet you, Paloma. Can I hold her?"

"Nice to meet you, Sol. Yes, of course."

I grabbed this fat little baby and inhaled her scent. I was young, but I couldn't wait to be a mother. I just loved kids, especially babies.

I looked over at Sawyer, who was intently watching me hold Sky. After a few more baby snuggles, I handed her back to Paloma.

"The house smells amazing. What are you cooking?"

"Oh. I'm making chile verde. Do you like to cook?"

I laughed. "No. I can't cook at all. I wish I could though. My mom's an amazing cook."

"Well, I can teach you."

I smiled. That would be nice. Would I ever see Paloma again? How long would this relationship or fall fling or whatever it was last with Sawyer?

"That would be great. I can help if you want."

"I'd like that."

Paloma handed Sky to Beck, and Sawyer made silly faces at Sky, and I just melted. He seemed to really like kids.

Stop, tripping Sol. This is a fling. You are not going to marry Sawyer and have his babies.

I joined Paloma in the kitchen. This place was gorgeous with a full view of downtown Kirkland and the water. I loved how Beck and Paloma were using this air show stop as a mini-vacation.

Paloma offered me a glass of sangria, which I readily accepted.

"¡Salud!"

"¡Salud!" We clinked our glasses.

Paloma's lips widened into a wry smile. "So, what's going on with you and Sawyer? Beck says he's never seen him so crazy about *one* girl."

She emphasized the word *one*. Yup. Got it. Sawyer was a manwhore, but he'd told me as much himself, so it was nothing new. Still, why was I letting that bother me?

"I don't know. I mean, he let me post a picture of him on Instagram and told me to write that he was my man. But we haven't talked about the future or anything like that. It's still so new."

"Are you going to Pensacola with him tomorrow?"

Sawyer was leaving tomorrow—hell, I had his entire schedule memorized. When he had invited me to Seattle, it had been in the spur of the moment. I didn't even have a plane ticket back to San Francisco since I'd flown here with Sawyer.

"I don't know. We haven't talked about it."

Paloma laughed. "Well, girl, you'd better talk about it, since it's like tomorrow. I was lucky Beck and I lived together for twelve weeks before he had to travel, but even that almost broke us. And to be honest, it did. I dumped him. But we worked it out. It's hard to start a relationship without spending normal time together that isn't on the road."

Her words hung heavy in the air. This was so unrealistic. Sawyer and I were living in a fantasy land.

I looked over at Sawyer, who was now playing on the floor with Sky. Who was this man? I had to get to know him in his own space. And that meant traveling with him to Pensacola tomorrow. If I spent some time with him in Pensacola before I went to Miami, I was sure we could decide if we wanted to take things further or end it now before someone—and by someone, I meant me—got hurt.

CHAPTER 21
SAWYER

After another incredible meal made with love by Paloma, Sol and I headed back to our hotel room. It would be our last night together in Seattle.

What was going to happen tomorrow?

I had invited her to Seattle on a whim because I'd wanted to get to know her better. And we had definitely bonded. I always had a great time with her regardless of what we were doing. She was stunning, sweet, and understanding. Yes, I had just claimed her as my woman in front of all of her followers, but everything was so new and so intense. We had literally spent every day together since we'd met. Was that normal? Was she getting sick of me?

I surprised myself by wanting to spend even more time with her. I didn't feel smothered. But maybe, especially since we weren't having sex, we should step back and take it slower. But selfishly I didn't want to let her go.

She stared at me as I drove. "What are you thinking about?"

"You."

She smiled. "Ah. I had a really great time with you and your friends tonight. Especially Paloma. I love her. She's fabulous."

"Yup, she is. Beck really lucked out finding her. I thought he was insane at first for dating Sky's nanny. But it worked out for them, and I'm happy for him."

"You're a good guy, Sawyer." She reached for my belt and unbuckled it.

"Babe, what are you doing?"

"Relax, Sawyer. You're a pilot. Just keep your eyes on the road." She loosened her seat belt and leaned over to the driver's seat. She placed her head in my lap and then slowly unbuttoned my pants.

I couldn't believe she was actually going to give me head in this car.

Fuck. This was so hot. For a virgin, she was a freak. I loved it.

She freed my cock from my pants. After a few quick kisses on the tip, she licked under my shaft.

I was rock hard. Every night this week, we had slept with our bodies next to each other, my cock pressed against her ass. It had almost been unbearable. I wanted her so bad.

"Stop teasing me, babe."

She let out a wicked little laugh that slayed me, then opened her mouth wide, and deep-throated my cock.

Jesus.

The cover of night hid our illicit encounter from the other drivers. I placed my hand on the back of her head, stroking her gorgeous hair as it made a blanket over my lap.

She began to suck harder and glided her other hand up and down my cock, increasing the tension. Pressure built in my balls as she kept edging me toward the point of no return. Emotions I didn't know I had flooded through me. How could this woman be so sexy, yet sweet? Wild, yet pure? Loving, yet tough?

And crazier yet, why did she like me?

Her lips made a tight seal around my tip. I was so close. I tried to push her off, not wanting to come in her mouth.

But she wouldn't release her grip with her hand or her mouth.

"Babe, stop. I'm going to come."

She paused for the briefest of moments to utter in a sultry voice, "Then come, Huck." She wrapped her mouth back around my cock.

Damn. A surge of pleasure overtook my body, and I came inside her hot mouth. She swallowed down every last drop of my cum, licked me clean, kissed my cock, and then sat back in her seat. I zipped my pants back up, grateful that we hadn't been caught by the cops.

Fuck.

I took a moment to catch my breath. "What was that for?"

She grinned. "I just like you. You're great, Sawyer. I don't really know what you want from me or where this is going, but I've had the best time with you."

"Me too, babe."

I paused. I'd considered suggesting we spend some time apart. I wanted to spend all my non-flying time with her but was afraid I'd somehow fuck up whatever we had going on.

Over the past week, I realized that I was capable of being in a relationship. I wanted to be there for someone and have someone miss me when I was gone. Someone who cared about me. I could make this work. I wanted Sol.

"Look, Sol. What I said the other night when Joy took that picture—"

Her beautiful face fell. "Oh, no worries. I get it. We were just in the moment."

I shook my head. "No. It's not that at all. I meant it. This is serious for me. It's not a fling. I really want to make this work."

She leaned over and kissed me on the cheek. "Me too. I know it can. I'm kind of obsessed with you. It's unhealthy really. If you had an Instagram account, I'd be stalking you."

I laughed. "Well, good thing I don't. I know that's your life, but I still don't give a shit about that stuff. I don't want people to worship me for what I look like, just for what I do."

She pursed her lips. I didn't want to hurt her feelings, but that was how I felt. I also believed Sol had so much more to offer the world than what she posted on social media. Maybe I could help her discover her true passion.

"So, should I buy a plane ticket back to San Francisco? I totally understand if you need to just unwind alone back at your place in Pensacola."

I reached over and grabbed her hand. "No, babe. I don't want to be alone. I want you to come to Pensacola with me."

She beamed. "I thought you'd never ask."

CHAPTER 22
SOL

Tonight was the night.

Sawyer and I had spent the last two nights at his house on base in Pensacola. I really loved it out here—the people were friendly, it was warm and sunny unlike San Francisco, and it wasn't as humid as I thought it would be. Sawyer had been showing me around town and even took some more Instagram pictures with me. I usually wasn't a beach girl, but I enjoyed relaxing in the sand and reading a book while Sawyer surfed.

But I'd made a decision this morning. I didn't want to wait any longer, and I didn't need to be in love. We were in a committed relationship. I was ready.

Sawyer kissed me on the forehead when I told him. "Are you sure? We don't have to. I'll wait for you."

"Yes, I'm sure. I'm excited."

He grinned and then drew me a bath. Then he poured me a glass of champagne and served me some strawberries.

He raised his flute to mine. The glasses clinked as he gave a toast. "To us."

"To us."

He fed me a strawberry and then walked out of the bathroom.

I slid into the bubbles and relaxed.

My mind raced. This was so romantic. *He* was so romantic. Truly a fantasy coming true. I had no doubts.

I sipped my champagne and tried to calm my nerves. After a few deep calming breaths, I finally emerged, slick and wet and ready for Sawyer.

Ready to give myself completely to him. I rubbed lotion all over my body and put on a white satin slip over my head. I took a look in the mirror and saw a sexy, beautiful woman staring back at me.

Sawyer had lit candles all around the room. He stood in front of the bed with wearing nothing but pajama bottoms. He had the most incredible body—a strong defined chest with tattoos, ripped arms, and a sexy V under his abs.

I stood there awkwardly for a second.

"You look so beautiful, babe." He pulled the straps of my slip down over my shoulders and let my slip fall to the floor, then he picked me up and carried me to the bed.

He kissed slowly down my face and nibbled at my earlobe. His breath on my collarbone caused heat to grow between my legs. I kissed him back, running my hands all over his tanned skin, pulling him closer to me.

He turned his attention to my breasts, slowly licking my nipples until he took one in his mouth and sucked on it.

I was dying for him.

Every kiss, every lick, every touch made the anticipation that much greater.

He settled in between my thighs and kissed my most sensitive spot. Over the past two weeks, I had been drowning in the pleasure that he gave me. Sawyer was so unselfish. He spoiled me, eating my pussy every chance he got, and I craved his tongue. He made me feel like a sexy woman.

My sex drive had gone from cautiously curious to insatiable, but I no longer wanted an appetizer. I wanted the main course.

I relaxed as Sawyer licked me, my breathing rapidly increasing.

"Babe, I'm ready. Please. Don't make me wait."

A wicked smile graced his face.

I took another deep breath. After years of waiting and wondering when I would lose my virginity, and who I would lose it to, the time had finally come. But I wasn't scared like I thought I would be or nervous like I'd been that night in San Francisco. I was thrilled—I couldn't wait.

He rolled the condom onto his delicious cock.

He pressed his chest into mine and stared into my eyes. One more sweet kiss on my lips, and then he slowly entered me.

"Ah." The pressure was so sweet and intense.

"You okay, babe?"

"Yup, don't stop."

He slid in a bit farther, inch by inch, closer to my soul. And then a wave of pain crashed over me.

I gasped.

His handsome face scrunched up. "Want me to stop?"

The beat of his heart vibrated against my chest. "No."

He slowly moved back and forth inside me. The pain was quickly being replaced by pleasure. We were finally one.

"How do you feel?"

"Amazing. Sawyer, don't hold back, make love to me. Please."

And that was exactly what he did.

He sped up his tempo all the while maintaining eye contact with me. I wanted to cry out—it felt so good, so bad, so right. Pleasure tinged with pain.

I just wanted more of this, more of him.

"I'm crazy about you, Sunshine."

Sunshine. Was this his new pet name for me? His words penetrated me as deep as his cock had. To my head, to my heart, to my soul.

And as much as this moment, this lovemaking meant to me, I couldn't help thinking it meant more to him. This wasn't casual sex. Would things change between us tomorrow?

He kissed my lips and my breasts as he thrust deeper inside of me.

I closed my eyes, just giving in to the moment, savoring every movement, every touch, every kiss.

"Babe, come here."

He pulled me up to a sitting position, and I wrapped my legs around him. We sat facing each other, eye to eye, soul to soul.

"Ride me."

I rode up and down on his cock, and at first, the pain from his size was almost too much to bear, but I forced myself to relax.

Sawyer was so loving with me. He maintained his gaze and kissed my nipples as I controlled our rhythm. The more I focused on Sawyer, the wetter I became. Slowly, I could feel the ecstasy build.

"That's it, baby."

He grasped my hips and guided my motion.

I could feel the pleasure come in waves, nothing like I had experienced before.

The intensity built, and I was sure I was going to burst. I had come before, but nothing had ever felt like this.

So pleasurable, so incredible, so loving, so sexy.

Sawyer's hands gripped my ass. I rubbed my clit on him as he sucked my nipple.

"You're the most beautiful woman I've ever met. And you're all mine. Come with me, babe."

My breath hitched, and the pleasure came back. I had to get out of my head and just feel, just be here, be in the moment.

And no one was better at making me do that than Sawyer.

He spoke in almost a whisper. "I'm falling so hard for you."

And with that, I closed my eyes and gave myself over to him, truly over. I had nothing left to hold back.

He thrust deeper inside of me as he sucked on my nipples, alternating between each one.

I screamed in pleasure.

"Oh oh oh oh!"

"Yeah babe, let go."

Joy rippled through my body as we came together, our bodies a sweaty, sexy mess.

I let out a long laugh, and he laughed too. He got up and ran to the bathroom to throw the condom away. When he returned, his eyes zeroed in on the blood on the sheets. A proud look graced his handsome face, but he didn't say anything about the stain. He climbed back into bed and held me closer than he had ever had before.

He pushed a lock of hair back from my face and kissed me.

"So, how was it?"

"Amazing! Everything I thought it would be and more. I want you to make love to me every day."

"That can be arranged."

He kissed me again. I hopped out of the bed and dashed to the bathroom. I looked at myself in the mirror. I felt stronger and sexier than I ever had.

Then my phone beeped.

I grabbed it—it was Kelli.

Kelli: I just emailed your flight information for Friday.

Fuck! Friday was in two days. I hadn't told Sawyer yet that I was heading to Miami, not that I thought he'd mind. I'd ask him to come with me, but there were strict rules in the contract about not bringing a boyfriend or spouse. I understood the brand's point—Sawyer would be a distraction.

I'd tell him tonight. But for now, I just wanted to bask in his love.

CHAPTER 23
SAWYER

Taking Sol's virginity had been one of the best nights of my life. We'd had sex four times yesterday. She couldn't get enough. Neither could I.

And I wish it hadn't meant so much to me, but the fact that she'd never been with another man, that I was the only man who ever made her come like that, drove me wild. I had an insane desire to protect her, a desire I'd never felt toward anyone but my brothers-in-arms.

Sol and I had made love in the morning and spent the day riding bikes. When we got home, I ran out to grab a pizza. I couldn't wait to drink a cold beer and chill with my woman.

My woman. I could hardly believe my life right now. Typically, I spent my rare time off hitting the bars, meeting a new woman every night.

But I couldn't think about anyone else but Sol.

The crazy thing was that I didn't even remotely miss that life. Sol was everything to me. I missed her when I was away from her even for a few minutes.

"Hey, Sunshine."

"Hey." She greeted me with a kiss. She was wearing these short little pajama bottoms, and I wanted to rip them off and devour her pussy.

I popped open a beer. Sol bit her lower lip and struggled to make eye contact. What was wrong? For a second, I thought she was going to break up with me.

"Oh, I've been meaning to tell you—I got this amazing opportunity the other week."

I exhaled, relieved that I'd been wrong. "Congrats. What is it?"

"A manager for some major brands has asked me to fly to Miami and take some pictures for his products."

I studied her face. "Why do you have to go to Miami?"

"That's where he's located."

He? "Who?"

She took out her phone and showed me the profile of some guy named Vidal Verity. This douche's Instagram was full of beautiful women in bikinis, on his yacht, and in his hot tub with his arms around them.

Oh, hell no.

Fuck. I'd never been someone's boyfriend before. I didn't want to come off as a controlling dick. But I was highly suspicious of some guy wanting to take pictures of Sol. I understood that this was her job, but she was so naïve and trusting. Hell, she flew to Seattle with me without even knowing me.

"When?"

She grimaced. "Tomorrow. Sorry, I knew about this last week, but I didn't know what was going on with us or if we'd still be dating so I didn't tell you."

Well, that was reassuring. But after the stunt Veronica pulled, I didn't blame her.

She'd followed me around for my job, so I was going to man up and do the same for her.

"That's fine. I have the day off. I'll fly you there. I can use my buddy's plane."

She shook her head. "No. That won't work. No significant others allowed."

My chest constricted. Nope. Not going to happen.

"Well then, you can tell him that you aren't going."

Her gaze narrowed at me. "What? This is my job, Sawyer. I'm not a child."

"No, you aren't a child. But you're my girlfriend. This guy could be a rapist. I read about this man once who was scamming models. It's suspicious that he won't let your boyfriend go. So, if I can't go with you, you're not going. That's final. You'll get other jobs."

Her voice raised. "Are you're kidding me right now. It's super legit. Kelli said—"

"Fuck Kelli. Sol, how fucking naïve are you? It's legit because you have a contract? You fucking told me yourself about that one guy who was trying to sext you. He had a contract, too. I'm not telling you that you can't work. I offered to go with you. But this guy even put in the contract 'no significant others allowed.' That's shady. The answer is no. You're not going."

She glared at me. "You can't tell me where I can and can't go."

I took a deep breath and forced myself to calm down. I needed to try another approach. She was so sweet and trusting. She always looked for the good in people, and I knew better than most that some people would do nothing but take advantage of someone like Sol. "Babe, are you serious right now? Do you know how sketchy this sounds? Some guy, who you've never met, wants you to fly alone to Miami to take pictures. You're actually entertaining this right now? He could be a sex trafficker."

"Christ, Sawyer, he's not a sex trafficker. Or a rapist. I mean, he has a ton of followers on Instagram."

I laughed. "Like that means anything. You know better than anyone that Instagram is all fake."

Her nostrils flared. Dammit—that had been the exactly wrong thing to say to her.

"Fuck you, Sawyer. I've worked my ass off to get organic followers. I know you don't respect what I do, but you could at least pretend."

"See, that's the difference between you and me, Sol. I don't pretend. I'm real. And my feelings toward you are one-hundred-percent real. I'm crazy about you. I just want to protect you."

"Wow. You're so fucking paranoid. Not everyone is out to have sex with me, and I don't need protecting. You just think the worst of everyone in my world. This is a legitimate job."

"Then call him right now and say that you feel more comfortable if your boyfriend comes with you. I'm not trying to interfere with your work. You won't even know I'm there. But I don't want you alone with this man. If you don't want me tagging along, that's fine, too. I trust you. But then I'm hiring you security."

She looked at me, and her hands shook. "I'm going, Sawyer. Alone. And honestly, I think we made a mistake here. You'll never accept what I do. I don't want to be with someone who tells me what I can and can't do. Who thinks my job and my life are jokes. I don't think this can work out."

My vision blurred. This couldn't be happening to me. No. Not now. Not when I'd fallen for her. Not when I . . .

"You're breaking up with me because I'm worried about your safety? And I don't think your job and life are jokes. But unlike everyone else in your life, I'm going to be honest with you and not blow smoke up your ass. Despite having over a million followers, you're so alone. You told me when we met that you don't have any close friends. You post about avocado toast, vanilla lattes, and sunsets, but you're so much more than that. You're smart; you're compassionate. You could be making a real difference in people's lives like you have in mine."

Her bottom lip quaked. "We haven't even known each other for more than two weeks, and you're telling me what to do. I don't like it."

I held her arms and forced her to look at me. "I just want you to be safe. All I'm asking is to go with you or for you to get security. Is that too much to ask?"

"That's not how these things are done."

I shook my head. "Sol, you live in la-la land with your unicorn lattes and mermaid bowls. There are some really evil people out there. I'm not saying he is, but you need to be safe."

"I'll be safe. But Sawyer, I'm going."

And with that, she stormed into the bedroom to pack. I downed my beer as my world closed in on me.

After twenty minutes, she emerged. "I'm going to stay in a hotel tonight. Maybe we can talk when I get back."

"If you come back."

She rolled her eyes. "Look, I hear what you are trying to say, and I appreciate your concern, but I can take care of myself. We can install an app on our phones to track each other. That way you'll know where I am."

"Is that what you think of me, Sol? That I'm some possessive boyfriend who needs to know where you are at all times? That's not it, at all. I just want you to be safe."

"I understand. But we can sync it, just in case."

I pushed my rage down and reluctantly agreed. I was so fucking pissed right now, I couldn't see straight.

Her Uber came to take her away. "Bye, Sawyer. I'll fly back here on Sunday. Then we can talk."

"Bye, Sol." She didn't even kiss me goodbye. Once she shut the door, I grabbed my beer bottle and threw it against the wall. The shards of glass shattered just like my heart. Would I ever see her again? Or would she be just another person in my life who left me?

CHAPTER 24
SOL

I felt so awful about my fight with Sawyer, but I wasn't going to allow him to control me.

I understood he was worried, but I had gone to hundreds of shoots and nothing had ever happened. Granted, most of them were local, and I usually had either Kelli or a stylist come with me, but I'd be fine. This was standard for my job.

Just as I arrived at the airport, an email popped up from Vidal.

Urgent, please call.

Great. I hoped everything was okay.

I called Vidal.

"Hi, Sol. Thanks for calling. We have an emergency."

Ugh. My heart sank. But millions of issues could come up with a shoot, so I needed to stay positive.

"Oh really? What happened?"

"Well, we need a special filming permit. I'd pay but the banks are closed, and I had my wallet stolen the other week. Pickpockets. Anyway, I'll reimburse you for sure, but if you could front the payment that would be great."

I had a sudden sinking feeling in the pit of my stomach.

My gut told me something was wrong. I wanted to call Kelli, but she was gone for the day, and I didn't want to bother her at home. I'd call Sawyer, but I'd been so awful to him, and I didn't want him to gloat about being right.

I closed my eyes. Maybe this made sense. I was aware that a shooting permit would be needed. Maybe Vidal really did have his wallet stolen. I'd lost my purse more times than I could count. And my phone.

This was fine. I would not freak out.

"Of course, I understand. Send me the information, and I'll pay it."

He exhaled. "Thank you, doll."

I cringed when he said *doll*. But that was how many photographers referred to models. There wasn't anything wrong with that term.

"You're welcome. Who's meeting me at the airport?"

"His name is Manny. Then he will take you to the warehouse to meet me."

The warehouse? Fuck. "You know, I was wondering if I could bring someone with me to the shoot. I would just feel safer."

"Now, doll. That is not what the contract says. You agreed—"

Fuck. Sawyer was right. Something was way off. I shouldn't have to feel uncomfortable. I had just been so angry that Sawyer had told me what to do that I hadn't listened to what he said.

"Well, you agreed to pay. The contract is void. I'm not coming."

I hung up the phone, not even waiting for his response.

I didn't feel sad. I felt relieved. But I was angry at myself.

I picked up the phone and called Sawyer. He answered on the first ring.

"Hey."

"Hey. Look, I'm sorry about last night. I think you were right. I'm still in Pensacola. Will you come get me at the airport?"

"I'm on my way."

Two Weeks Later

After the Vidal situation, I'd pulled back from social media. It turned out that he had scammed many other influencers. And even worse, he had sexually assaulted a few women. Many others had all been bilked out of money from fraudulent last-minute permit fees. I was hopeful that I could save at least one person from my fate by telling my story. So, I posted about it and had received an outpouring of support. But unfortunately, Vidal had not been found.

Sawyer hadn't once rubbed my face in the fact that he had been right. He had apologized for telling me what to do and promised to work on his communication skills. He'd never been in a relationship before, so he was struggling on how to navigate his position in my life. And I got that. On my end, I promised to calmly listen to his concerns and try not to overreact. He was worth it, so I was happy to take the time to assure him that I wasn't going anywhere.

Last week, I had accompanied Sawyer to Minnesota, which was absolutely beautiful. We had a wonderful time, and I had met the nicest people.

We spent Sawyer's non-flying time sightseeing, but I no longer felt the need to hire a local photographer everywhere I went. I was still trying to figure out my true passion.

This week, we were back in Pensacola. Tonight, Sawyer had made me an amazing steak dinner. He was a great chef, which was wonderful because I was no Paloma. All night throughout dinner, a hunger of a different kind grew inside me. There was no more doubt. I loved Sawyer. Truly loved him like I'd never loved another soul.

I had to tell him.

He poured me a glass of wine, and I stared at him. He was so handsome. That first night at the Chinese restaurant he'd definitely felt as uncomfortable in my world as I'd felt in his. But over the past month, we'd grown together. He didn't flinch when I took pictures of our meals, and I didn't complain when he took me to a greasy burger joint.

We weren't alike—no, we were way different. But somehow, we made sense.

"Babe, what's up? You look distracted."

I smiled. "I have something to tell you."

His brow furrowed. "What is it? Please don't tell me you have another gig that you have to go to alone."

"No, it's nothing like that. I learned my lesson."

"Then what is it?"

I looked into his beautiful eyes. "I love you, Sawyer."

A blank look graced his face, followed by a deafening silence.

Definitely not the reaction I was looking for. "Sawyer, did you hear me? I love you."

"You sure?"

What kind of response was that? "Yes, I'm sure. I love you. I know it's only been a month, but you're wonderful. I have changed and grown so much since we met. I'm madly in love with you."

"Cool."

Cool? His tone was a bit icy, and honestly, my heart hurt not hearing him say he loved me back. I didn't say it for him to repeat it, but even so, I felt he loved me.

I silently pouted. After dinner, we normally turned on Netflix and then made love all night.

But this night was different.

He put on his shoes and looked at me coldly.

"I have to take care of some business. I'll be back later."

I paused. "Business? A night flight?"

"I'm behind on some admin crap since we've been spending so much time together."

I eyed him hard. Sawyer was never behind on any flight reports. He was the best pilot and super organized with paperwork, unlike me. Even Beck had complimented Sawyer on his attention to detail. Even worse, he was trying to blame me for not having time to work, which was ridiculous. I never once interfered with this job.

But I understood he needed to process what I said to him. I was not going to freak out, yet. "Okay. I love you."

"Don't wait up."

Damn, he didn't even kiss me goodbye. That was a first.

My heart constricted and sadness overtook me.

I walked into the bedroom and took out a scrapbook that I had been making. It had all our pictures together—ones I hadn't posted on social media. Every meal we ate was depicted here, including the dumplings.

I looked at a picture of him looking at me with love in his eyes.

It didn't matter to me that he wouldn't admit it.

I knew he loved me.

And for now, that would have to be enough.

CHAPTER 25
SAWYER

I walked out of my place, got into my Tesla, and drove straight to the nearest bar.

Sol loved me?

What the fuck? How could she love me? She didn't even know me.

I never wanted that. Ever. I'd told her from day one that I didn't do relationships. I had her sweet, tight, virgin pussy so strong on my brain that I couldn't think straight. I should've never asked her to be my girlfriend.

I don't want that life. I don't want to be responsible for anyone but myself.

I called Beck.

"What's up?"

"I just wanted to make sure that you never changed my orders."

Beck paused. I didn't want him questioning me. Not tonight.

"I haven't finalized them yet. I thought you might reconsider. Maybe you could get stationed with me in San Diego. Paloma and Sol really seemed to like each other."

"I don't want to go to San Diego. I want to go to Japan."

"Are you okay, Huck? Did you guys break up?"

"No, man the opposite. She just told me she loved me."

"Ah. And you freaked out. Look, you aren't going to fuck this up. You're a better man when you're with her. A good man, in fact. And you're happy with her. You don't have to propose or anything. Just see where it goes."

I'd had enough of this shit. "Look, Daly. I don't need you or Sol psychoanalyzing me. I never led anyone on. I don't want to settle down. Finalize my fucking orders."

"You're making a mistake, man. I can tell you love her."

"No, Beck. You made a mistake thinking I could change. You've been right about me from day one. I'm a jackass. I don't care about Sol. I don't care about you. I only care about myself."

I hung up the phone. I arrived at the bar and ordered a shot of bourbon. I had to end it with Sol. No hard feelings, but it, whatever it was, had run its course. I didn't want to be with her anymore. I just wanted to be alone.

CHAPTER 26
SOL

I paced around Sawyer's place. He'd never once gone out all night and not returned my calls. I must've spooked him by telling him I loved him.

I waited up for him and tried to distract myself with shows on Netflix. I had to talk to him tonight. I couldn't sleep anyway.

He finally waltzed in the door at two thirty in the morning, liquor on his breath. I was at least relieved that he'd taken an Uber home and hadn't driven drunk.

I wasn't going to nag. He didn't need accusations. And I was certain he hadn't cheated on me. He wouldn't stoop that low.

I greeted him with a kiss. "Hey, you okay? Do you want to talk?"

"Don't start with me, Sol."

Well, then. I wasn't going to let him talk to me like that. "What does that mean? Why are you acting like this? Because I told you I love you? I do love you, even though you're being a major dick right now."

"Why do you love me?"

"Why? So many reasons. I love the way you make me feel. How you see through me. How I can relax and be myself around you. I can't do that with anyone else in my life. I love the sweet and kind way you interact with your fans. I love the way you command an airplane. I love the way you protect me. I love the way you kiss me."

He turned away. "Well, this has gone on too long. I was clear with you from day one. I don't want to lead you on. I like you a lot, but I don't love you, Sol. This isn't real to me. You were a challenge. We had our fun, but I have orders to Japan next year. Unaccompanied. I think we should just end it now before I hurt you further."

I blinked back the tears that were forming. He didn't mean those awful words coming out of his mouth. I knew he loved me. He was just afraid. He'd never been in love.

"That hurts, but no, I won't let you get rid of me. You're trying to hurt me to protect yourself. I've seen the real you, Sawyer. You aren't an asshole. And I know you love me by your actions."

His brow furrowed. "Didn't Veronica teach you anything? I *am* that guy. I just wanted to fuck you, Sol. To be your first. To pop your cherry—I'd never been with a virgin. It was a challenge, and it was great. But I don't care about you. I don't care about anyone but myself. I'm a selfish prick."

Oh, how I hated his words, but he was lashing out. "Why are you pushing me away? Why are you lying to me? You love me, Sawyer. Admit it."

"I don't! I told you from day one this would never ever work. I'm in the military. I'm a Marine, a Blue Angel, a fighter pilot. I don't want a wife, I never did."

"I'm not asking to marry you tomorrow. But everything was going so great, so I told you I loved you and you just flipped. That's not a coincidence. I should've waited. I knew that you couldn't handle it. So much for all your 'I'm so real' bullshit. I'm the one who's being real now, and you can't handle it."

He scoffed. "Whatever, Sol. You're using me, too."

"Really, how so? Enlighten me."

"I'm your hot Instagram pilot boyfriend. You love to take pictures of me and parade me around, but you don't want to know the real me. What happened to me."

My voice dropped. "What are you talking about?"

His fists clenched, and his face reddened.

"How my mom left me, how her boyfriends, how they . . . " His voice trailed off.

His silence was deafening.

I walked over to him. "What, Sawyer? What did they do to you?"

"They beat me. They left me outside to rot while they were inside fucking my mom. They *touched* me, dammit. And I was so lonely, I craved their attention. Is that what you want to hear? I hate myself. I don't know how to be a good man. I will cheat on you. I will. I fuck to numb the pain. It's only a matter of time. I'm not who you think I am. I told you I'm a bad man, but you wouldn't listen, just like you aren't listening right now."

My heart shattered into a million pieces. This broken boy didn't believe he was worthy of love.

"You're everything I think you are and more. You're kind and smart and loving. I see you with the kids who come to the show. I'm so sorry all those awful things happened to you, Sawyer, but you beat the odds and succeeded. You're the strongest man I've ever met. You deserve love, Sawyer. And I love you dammit."

"No. I don't want you to love me. You need to go."

"Are you breaking up with me?"

He gave me a blank stare. "Yeah, that's exactly what I'm doing."

I blinked back the sudden rush of tears in my eyes and tried to remain calm.

"I know you love me. If we could just take a step back—"

"No, I don't. I just want you to leave."

"You don't mean that. We were planning a winter getaway earlier today before I told you I love you, and now you want to dump me? You *love* me."

"Dammit, Sol! Why do you have to be so narcissistic all the time? You only see what you want to see. Your world isn't reality. You live in la-la land. Well, the world isn't perfect, it's a fucking mess like me, and you know it."

"At least I'm not afraid of putting myself out there and getting hurt, because getting hurt only means that you tried to get the best reward—which is love."

"If I fall in love with you, then what? You will just leave me."

"I will never leave you."

"Everyone leaves me."

"I won't. My parents have been married for twenty-four years, and they didn't leave. I stick—I'm like peanut butter. Just let me love you."

He took a moment and stared at me. For a moment, I thought he would come back to me, but he turned around, and just like that, he slipped away.

"No. I can't. I don't want to. You need to go."

My compassion turned to rage. "I never expected you to be a coward, Sawyer. Now I see you for who you are. You're nothing more than a scared little boy. I'm scared too. I'm such a mess with not knowing my purpose in life right now. But together we can be whole, and I love you, dammit."

"I don't love you."

"Keep telling yourself that. So now what? Are you going to go back to womanizing? Call Veronica?"

"Yeah, something like that."

"You're better than that."

"No, I'm not."

I looked at his blue eyes, and they were icier than they had ever looked before. It was as if his heart had just slammed the door on me just as soon as I'd found a way in.

Sawyer was right. I had to leave.

I went into the bedroom and packed my things. Thirty minutes later, I walked out to the living room. Sawyer was sitting on the sofa.

I leaned down and kissed his forehead. "Bye, Huck. I love you, and you're the best thing that ever happened to me."

I called an Uber and went to the airport, where I bought a first-class ticket back to San Francisco.

Back to my perfect fake life. Back to where I didn't have to feel anything.

CHAPTER 27
SAWYER

One month later

I was back on the air show circuit. I hadn't called Sol once. I was such an asshole. I hated myself. But it was better this way.

But not calling didn't mean that I wasn't thinking about her.

It was quite the opposite. I was a fucking mess. The only time I could concentrate was when I was in the air. But the second I touched down, all I could think about was Sol.

And she had been right—I did love her.

But it didn't matter. We weren't right for each other. She wanted a traditional life. To get married like her parents. Have kids. The dog and the picket fence. I didn't want that. I wanted to travel. I needed to be free to fly.

I hadn't even fucked anyone else. I had completely lost my game, not that I wanted to hook up. After having meaningful sex with Sol, my regular one-night stands just didn't appeal to me.

But tonight, I was going to get back in the game.

We were in Michigan, one of my favorite stops on the tour.

And more importantly, I'd get to see Miss Cherry.

Five years ago, after Lila had been crowned Miss Cherry, we had holed up together for three wild nights. I hadn't even been an Angel yet, but I had come that year to see the show when I was in town. Lila and I had been on fire. We barely came up for air. She was a wildcat. And our chemistry was off the chain.

She was just what I needed to get over Sol.

I texted Miss Cherry, and she met up with me at the hotel bar. She still looked amazing—long red hair with matching red lipstick.

"Hey, Sawyer. Don't you look sexy? Did you miss me? I missed you."

I cringed. No, I hadn't. I missed Sol.

"Sit down. I ordered you a drink."

She grabbed my thigh, but I pushed her hand off. What was wrong with me? I couldn't even handle another woman touching me. I needed another drink.

"I'll skip the drink. I'll do tequila shots off your abs later. Why don't we go back to the hotel now? I just want to suck your cock."

Whoa. Normally, I'd be turned on by her aggression, but this time, it felt cheap. "What's the rush? Let's hang out a bit. How've you been?"

She rolled her eyes. "Dammit, Huck. I don't have all night. I couldn't find a sitter for my son, so he's waiting in the lobby. So, let's get on with it. We both know what we want."

I recoiled from her, and a bitter taste pooled in my mouth. Her son? He was *here*? Waiting for her to fuck me so he could go home and go to sleep?

Oh my god. What am I doing? Who have I become?

My skin grew clammy, and I became disorientated like I'd done one too many flips in my plane. Instead of seeing Miss Cherry in front of me, I saw my mom.

What the fuck.

I snapped myself out of it. I needed to get out of here. Back to Sol. Beg her to take me back. She had been right about me. I was afraid.

And I did love her.

But first, I needed to do something.

"I want to meet your son."

"What? Why?"

"I just do. I have something for him. Take me to him, okay?"

She shrugged her shoulders, and we headed to the lobby in silence.

Sitting alone, playing on an older model phone was a boy about the age of four. When he saw his mom, he shuddered.

"I'm sorry, Mama. I didn't disturb nobody. I was quiet."

"Stop talking. My friend wants to meet you."

My boyhood passed before my eyes. Sitting in lobbies, dropped off at friends' houses and forgotten, sitting outside until it was pitch black outside, each time waiting for my mom to entertain her friends.

But then I looked closer at this boy. This blond-haired lad with light-blue eyes and a sad smile.

It couldn't be.

I whispered to Lila, "How old is he?"

"Four."

My chest constricted. Four. I had slept with her five years ago.

I took a step back. Could this boy be my son? The math worked out.

"Lila, could he be my kid?"

She looked at me with a cold-stone stare. "I don't know. Maybe. I was with a lot of guys at that time."

My world was closing in on me. "How could you not tell me that I could be a father? You have my number. We used condoms. I *always* use condoms." Without fail. Because I never, ever wanted to bring a child into the world and abandon him the way my father abandoned me.

"Well, I wasn't sure. I wasn't going to ask a bunch of men to take DNA tests." She looked at her boy, without a single hint of maternal love. "If he's yours, you can take him."

"Wait, what? You want to give away your *son*?"

"Hey. I said *if* he's yours. I'm struggling really bad right now. I don't have time for him. I don't have close family to help out with him, and I want to travel. I never wanted to be a mother."

I couldn't believe what I was hearing. "How could you just offer to give him up? Don't you love him?" I raised my voice, and I realized that I was yelling at my mom as much as I was yelling at Lila.

"Hey, you have no idea what this has been like for me. Being a parent sucks. I wish I'd never had him. If I had figured out who his dad was years ago, I would've given up my parental rights then and there. But I didn't. I never thought it was you because we used protection, but you're right, he does look like you. The summer that I was crowned Miss Cherry, I was with so many men. His dad could be anyone. But if he's your boy and you want to raise him, be my guest. I want my freedom back. I'd never hurt him, but I'm not cut out to be a mom."

I never prayed. Ever. But I made a silent prayer that this boy was really my son.

"What's his name?"

"Neil."

Neil. Like Neil Armstrong, the first man to walk on the moon.

Was this a sign?

"Can I talk to him?"

"Knock yourself out."

I knelt down next to him, this little boy who could possibly be my son. "Hey, buddy. My name is Sawyer. I'm a Blue Angel. Do you know what that is?"

His eyes widened. "You fly in those crazy planes and do flips?"

"Yes. Would you like to see my plane?"

"Really? You'd take me?"

"Yes. We'll go tomorrow. Until then, I have something for you."

I handed him a small metal Blue Angel plane I had stashed in my pocket. He beamed.

"Thank you! Mama, look!"

Lila ignored him, and my throat burned.

"You're welcome. I'll see you tomorrow."

I stood up, my mind racing.

"Hey, do you have his DNA on file?"

"Yeah, I did 23andMe to try to find his dad. No luck."

Wait, my DNA was on 23andMe, as well. I'd tried to find my own dad but had never found any leads. "I have mine uploaded. We would've matched. Can we check again?"

And there in the lobby, on our phones, we compared DNA test results. It was sadly not a match. A deep wave of disappointment washed over me.

But this boy needed me.

And quite possibly, I needed him more.

Lila shrugged. "Well, too bad. I may put him in foster care. I just need a break."

I took her hand. "Would you seriously have given him to me if I was his bio- dad?"

She shrugged. "Yeah, why not? You're a military pilot. I could've gotten back child support. He doesn't even have healthcare. But you're not, so I'm shit out of luck. I can never catch a break."

Catching a break would be giving up her son? How could she be so callous about him? But then again, my mom hadn't cared about me either.

"Well, what's changed? What if . . ." I couldn't believe I was about to say this, but I continued. "What if I wanted to adopt him? I don't care that he's not biologically mine. He needs someone who loves him. My mom didn't want me either. And I knew. It was painful."

Her jaw dropped open. "You would honestly raise a child who wasn't yours? I'm confused. You want to be with me and be his stepdad?"

Not just no, but hell no. Though I did realize that I must've been drawn to her in the past because she reminded me of my own mother. Beck was right—I did need therapy.

"No, Lila. I don't want to be with you. And I'm sorry I texted you tonight. I'd been seeing someone up until recently, and I fell in love with her. But I got scared, so I ghosted her. I didn't realize that until now. She makes me want to be a better person. But when I saw your little boy, I had an epiphany. I overcame all these obstacles in my life, not to be a Blue Angel, but to help other people. And I want to help your son. And . . ."

I took a deep breath.

I had to do this. Five minutes ago, she was willing to give this boy to me based on a DNA test. She was considering foster care. And I knew from our nights together, she liked to get high.

Who knew where this boy would end up? He could be beaten, neglected, or molested, just like I had been. I may not be his biological dad, but I was meant to be placed in his path.

This was exactly why I had become a Blue Angel. I just hadn't known it.

Until now.

"If you're serious about wanting to give him up for adoption or place him in foster care, I'd like to raise him. You can still see him whenever you want. But he needs a stable home."

She hugged me and began to cry. "Sawyer Roberts. You truly *are* an Angel. I knew you were a great man the second I met you. Honestly, I just want to be free. Move to the Virgin Islands. Reclaim the last five years. Find myself. If you're serious, you'd be a lifesaver. To him and me both. He's a good boy. I wish I didn't resent him. God knows I've tried to love him, but I just don't have it in me to love him the way a mother should."

Her words crushed me. Had my own mom resented me?

"I'm serious. We can figure out what we need to do legally. I'll even pay for the attorney's fees." I looked over at Neil. "Meet me here tomorrow, and I'll take him to see my plane."

I said good night to Neil and then went to my room, alone.

And I immediately made plans to go get Sol back.

CHAPTER 28
SOL

Normally, the view of the bridge from my balcony calmed me, but now all I could see was Sawyer.

Sawyer everywhere. Flying overhead. Making my heart soar. Drowning me in ecstasy.

Over the past month, I'd picked up the phone so many times and called him, but he'd never answered.

Maybe he'd blocked me?

But I didn't regret what I had done or what I had said to him. Maybe he was right—it would never work out. He was in the military; he would deploy, maybe he would cheat on me.

But in my heart, I knew it could work out. And we could be happy. Together.

On my end, I'd told Kelli I needed a break. She said that wasn't possible, so I fired her. And my followers dropped.

And that was how I learned I was truly alone.

I'd been feeling alone for years, with no real friends to call, and no one who really cared about me. Sure, Raine did, but she wasn't local, and she was almost always busy. I'd been so focused on my followers and my fake life that I had never really felt this emptiness before.

Hollow.

Numb.

Shallow.

I scrolled through my phone and couldn't even think of anyone to call. Not a single person I could invite to coffee. No family to call and say hi—my parents were off traveling on another one of their cruises.

This time they hadn't even said goodbye.

I didn't even have a pet. The only time I'd even considered getting a pet was when I wanted to adopt this odd-eyed cat I'd seen. He was gorgeous—one golden eye and one blue eye. Why had I wanted him? Was it because I wanted a companion? Wanted to save his life from a high-kill shelter?

No. I wish I could say that, but it would've been a lie.

The only reason I'd wanted that cat was because I believed I could make him an Instagram star and grow my following.

And now I had lost everything.

No wonder Sawyer didn't love me. He saw right through me. I was a joke.

The only way I even knew what Sawyer was up to was by following the #blueangels hashtag on Instagram and occasionally seeing him tagged in other people's photos.

I was so pathetic.

I didn't have a clue what to do.

I tried to get a hold of myself, but I burst into tears. There had to be someone else I could talk to, someone who would understand my anxiety, but I couldn't think of anyone. The irony of my life was that I had one million followers and not a single friend in the world.

I went into the bathroom and drew myself a warm bath, adding a capful of bubbles. Here I had these beautiful things—a soaking tub, a driftwood bath caddy, and luxurious spa essentials. But I took little joy in my life anymore.

I just wanted to be liked for me. For who I was, not what I could do for someone or how I could promote his business. I wanted to be liked in my grungy sweats with no makeup and no filters. Like Sawyer liked me.

I was about to slip into the bubbles and sob when I heard a distant song.

"You've Lost That Loving Feeling."

My pulse accelerated. Oh my god! It couldn't be.

I wrapped a towel around me and sprinted to the door. I looked through the peephole and Sawyer was standing outside, in his uniform, serenading me.

I couldn't even move, I was frozen.

"Sol, open up. It's me."

CHAPTER 29
SAWYER

Sol stood in front of me in one of my old T-shirts I'd given her and some baggy sweats with tears running down her face. How could I have ever left her?

"What are you doing here?"

"Sol, I love you. I'm so sorry about how I behaved. You were right about me. I was scared. I was a total fucking coward. I didn't believe you could really love me. But this last month without you has been the worst month of my life. I missed you so much, babe. And I swear to you, I haven't been with anyone else. I love you. Please forgive me."

She blinked and wiped her eyes with her hand. "What? No. You were right. I'm a fucking mess. Why would you love me? I'm a narcissist. I'm fake. You deserve better than me. I should be apologizing to you."

I wrapped my arms around her. "No, you're everything. You're beautiful and patient and loving and sweet and smart. I didn't even know how much I loved you until you were gone."

"Well, that was an act. For my followers. I have no friends. Even my parents never see me. I have no one, Sawyer. At least you have your squad. Declan and Beck love you. I'm fake. No one knows me—I don't even know who I am."

I held her as tightly as I could. "I do, Sol, I do. I love the way your lip crinkles when you are mad and the way you tug your hair when you are nervous. I love the way you put me in my place when I'm an asshole and the way you worry about me when I'm flying. I love you, Sol. Not Solana San Francisco. Not your fake-ass pictures, but I love you."

She sobbed in my arms. "I hate myself, Sawyer, I do. You have a purpose in life. You're a fucking hero, and I do nothing. You were right about me the first day we met. I'm a joke, a fucking joke. You deserve better than me."

Hearing her say those words gutted me. She was every-thing to me, yet she felt so empty. And instead of being there for her, I had added to her anxiety. I didn't deserve her.

"Don't say that. You totally changed me. Before I met you, I never wanted any relationship. I just fucked to feel good, to numb the pain, but I never felt anything, Sol. Nothing, until you. You made me feel alive, more alive than being in that fucking plane. I'm a new man because of you. I love you."

And finally, she broke. After all that denial and emotion, she wrapped her arms around me, kissing me, healing me with her touch.

"God, I'm sorry. I'm a wreck. I love you so much. You gutted me when you dumped me. I had never been so sure of anything. I can't believe you are back here."

I kissed my woman and vowed this time to never let her go. No matter what.

I threw her down on her sofa. Every time we'd had sex it had been so sweet and loving. But this time, I wanted to show her how much I loved her, how much I needed her, how she was my whole world.

I took off my clothes, undressed her, and climbed on top of her. My mouth covered hers, and our kisses were almost manic, insatiable. I couldn't get enough. I rubbed her pussy, and she was soaking wet.

I quickly rolled on a condom, grabbed my cock, and plowed into my baby. She groaned when I took her deep. God, she was still so fucking tight. I was worried she wouldn't like my roughness, my urgency, my desire, but Sol attacked me back, gripping my ass, urging me deeper into her.

I looked into her eyes. "I love you so fucking much."

"I love you too."

I fucked her harder, faster, as I sucked on her tits. Her breath sped up, and my baby was so close. I rubbed her clit and slammed into her over and over, again and again until she came all over my cock.

Sol had been right—sex was the best when you were in love.

After we'd recovered, I threw the condom in the trash and sat back on the sofa.

I pulled her to me and stroked her hair.

"Sol, I need to tell you something."

A look of horror crossed her face. "Are you still going to Japan?"

I shook my head. "No, I changed my orders to San Diego. I wanted to live near Beck and Paloma. I'm hoping you will move down with me."

"Of course, I will. What changed your mind?"

"You. I want to be with you. I don't want to deploy. As an Angel, I have my pick of duty station. We will have three years together there while I train young pilots."

She beamed. "Wow. That will be cool."

I exhaled. I needed to tell her the truth. "Also, I need to tell you something else."

"What?"

"If this scares you or you don't want to be a part of my life, I understand. But I need to be honest."

She held my hand. "Tell me. Do you have a kid?"

Man, she could read me like a book. "It's not what you think. There's this boy, but he's not my biological son. It's a long story. But he reminds me of me. I want to adopt him. But I need you to know that this is not why I'm getting back together with you. You're young. If you aren't ready to be a mom, that's fine. We can take our time and even live separately if you want. I don't want to be with another woman. I can raise him on my own if I have to. The adoption will take six months to get finalized. But I want to be his father."

She looked at me with tears in her eyes. Fuck, I screwed up again. I should've told her before we'd made love.

"Sawyer, I didn't think it was possible, but I love you even more."

CHAPTER 30
SOL

few months later

A I'd settled in quite nicely in Sawyer's home in Pensacola. We still planned to move to San Diego, but his orders were a few months away.

Sawyer was in the process of adopting Neil, though unfortunately due to interstate adoption rules, the little boy still resided in Michigan. Sawyer and I flew up every week on his days off. He was the sweetest little boy, and I was blessed to have him in my life. If Sawyer proposed to me, I would happily raise Neil.

Lila wanted to terminate all parental rights and not have any visitation. I couldn't fathom wanting to turn my back on my child, but I truly believed all women had the freedom to choose any path they wanted. I didn't judge Lila. She had never wanted a baby and had done the best she could. But after hearing Sawyer talk about his own mom, I realized that some women weren't cut out to be mothers. And that was okay. I was just grateful that Sawyer wanted to step up and give this little boy the happy home that Sawyer had never had.

As for me, I had completely retooled my life. I'd applied for graduate school. I wanted to be a Marriage and Family Therapist. Help people like Sawyer. People like Neil. People like me.

After a long social media break, I picked up my phone. But this time it was different. I was wearing sweats and a Blue Angel T-shirt.

I didn't have a hint of makeup on, my extensions were long gone, and I had even put on some weight since I was no longer consumed with how I would look on camera.

It didn't matter to me at all.

All that mattered was that Sawyer loved me the way I was.

Just Sol.

Hi Guys!

I know you're used to seeing me dolled up and glammed, but this is me.

No filter. I wanted to tell you all that everything you had seen in my feed was fake.

I mean the food was real, but I spent hours posing it and even longer doing my makeup. But that isn't real—a picture-perfect life doesn't exist.

The only thing left is my true feelings, and I have a confession to make.

When I met Sawyer, all I cared about was my image. It was more important for me to get more followers than be happy. But then, I fell in love.

I love him. I love Captain Sawyer Roberts. But this fake life got in the way of real-life feelings. So, don't be me. Live in the moment. Get off your phone. Go have coffee with a friend. Go hike. Go read a book. And tell someone you love them.

Peace and love. Sol

CHAPTER 31
SAWYER

When my plane touched down from my final show, Sol was in the crowds cheering for me.

In the past, when I'd returned from deployment, I'd never had anyone waiting for me. No one came to my graduation at Annapolis, because no one loved me.

But seeing Sol standing there in a long, flowing dress with a big grin on her face, I knew I had something now I'd never had before.

I had a family.

Time to make it official.

I'd thought of a million way to propose to Sol, but she deserved a grand gesture.

Something Instagram-worthy. I had arranged for someone to film it as well so she could post it to her followers.

I ran to Sol, and she leaped into my arms.

My mouth took hers, and we kissed for what seemed like forever.

I'd had this planned since we got back together.

"Babe. I have to go back up to make one more run in my plane really quick, and then we can go home."

"Really? You've never done that before."

"Yeah. It's a special flight. Promise me you'll watch."

"Of course."

I kissed her. The last kiss I would ever give my girlfriend.

I jumped back in the cockpit and took off. I had plotted this out meticulously.

But hell, if I could do a flight path in the shape of a dick, I could definitely write will you marry me.

I accelerated. Looping to the left and to the right, I even dotted the i.

Though I'd never felt sick from the G-Force, this time a wave of nausea passed through me.

There. It was done. No more turning back.

I turned the plane around and landed.

Once safely touched down, Sol came running to me.

"Are you serious? Is this some stunt?"

I climbed out of the cockpit, took the ring out of my zippered pocket and dropped to my knee.

Tears welled in her eyes.

"Solana Sanchez, I love you and don't want to ever be without you. Will you marry me?"

"Yes, yes, of course. I love you, Sawyer."

I slipped the ring on her finger.

Mine. All mine.

The San Francisco fog blanketed Mount Tam, but I wasn't chilly. My body was burning up from nerves—I was about to see my bride.

Beck punched me in the arm. "Never thought I'd be standing here next to you on your wedding day. You've come a long way, buddy. I'm happy for you. And not to sound like a condescending prick, but I'm proud of you too."

I hated to admit it, but those words meant the world to me. I didn't have a father figure, no one to call me out on my bullshit. Beck was the closest thing I had in my life to a strong male role model. Had Beck not forced me to take Sol on that first flight, I wouldn't be here today.

Our son, Neil, stood by my side. The adoption still wasn't finalized, but the judge had signed off on him living with us. Since Sol and I were getting married, she was going to adopt him as well. And Sol was amazing with him. So patient and loving. Seeing her with him made me love her even more.

Even so, it had been a hard adjustment for Neil. He was quiet and scared at first. We'd enrolled him in the best preschool in our area, and he was also seeing a therapist. I hadn't heard from Lila, but that was unsurprising. She'd thanked us for adopting her son and had just wanted to move on. I felt bad for Neil when he asked about her, knowing how conflicted I'd felt about my own mother at that age. But I knew that with time and love, he would thrive with us.

I was now stationed in San Diego, and Sol had moved down to live with me. The SoCal beach vibe suited her well—plenty of beautiful beaches to take pictures of sunsets and waves, though her business model had changed. Instead of just posting pictures of avocado toast all day, Sol had switched the focus of her blog and social media to finding happiness through real connection. She had also been accepted to graduate school and would start next fall. I was so damn proud of her.

Now, where was she?

After an agonizing wait, Sol walked down the aisle, escorted by her father. We hadn't spent too much time with her family—they were always gone. I was shocked by how distant they were, but maybe that would change in time. At least Sol and I both knew how we wanted to raise Neil and any other kids we planned to have one day.

Once Sol was in focus, I melted at the sight of my beautiful bride. She was simply stunning. And I couldn't believe she was mine.

We recited our vows, and I held her hands and gazed into her eyes.

"I love you, Sol."

"I love you, too, Sawyer."

The preacher announced, "You may now kiss the bride."

I gave her the most passionate kiss. Solana Roberts. My wife.

With Sol and Neil, I now had the family I craved, that I hadn't even known I'd wanted. And for the first time in my life, I was complete.

Thank you for reading ***Blue Moon***!

I hope you loved Sawyer and Sol. Hungry for more Blue Devils? Read Declan & Storm's love story in ***Blue Thunder,*** preorder now.

Blue Thunder

Nails on a chalk board. A newborn's first cry. The heavy metal that drowns out my pain. The gasp of his last breath. The sobs of my guilt.

These are the sounds that destroy me, ring through my head, turn our dreams into nightmares. No matter how much vodka I drink nor how many pills I take, I will never forget the songs you sang to me, the strum of your guitar, your voice when you first told me you loved me.

But I said nothing.

Nothing about how much I craved you, nothing about your brother, the man who destroyed us, nothing about my pain.

And now all I have left is the sound of silence.

I am no longer the innocent girl you once loved. While you achieved your goals soaring in the air, life squashed mine down on land. You want me back, but I refuse to let you in for lightning pulses through my veins and even the power of your blue thunder can never calm my storm.

Order ***Blue Thunder*** Now

And sign up for my ***newsletter*** to find out about my latest books.

If you loved Blue Moon, you'll love the thrilling, dark, and sensual Trident Code series. **INVINCIBLE** is available now.

Like Navy SEAL cowboys and rescue dogs? Preorder **Wild Love**, the first book in a new series now.

And don't miss my Beauty & The Beast retelling, **The Beauty & The BEAST,** available now.

Want to connect with me? Stalk me on **Instagram,** like my **Facebook page,** or join my Facebook group, **Alana Albertson's Allstars** for exclusive giveaways and previews of my latest books.

I would love your help in spreading the word about my books, including telling a friend. Reviews help sell books. If you liked my book, would you please consider leaving a review for ***Blue Moon***?

XOXO
Alana

ACKNOWLEDGMENTS

I WOULD LIKE TO THANK

Wander for taking this amazing picture.

Aria for your brilliant cover.

Kelli for your insight to these characters.

Dana for saving this book when I was in a bind.

Chris for fleshing this out.

Craig for your patience with the changing ARC dates.

Nicole for nagging me to finish it and your pretty teasers.

Stasia for your beta. #teamcherry

Lisa for listening to me whine about this book.

Roger for taking care of me when I was too sick to write.

My boys for being the best part of my day.

My fans for reading my books, even though I know you all want Snow 2 (it's coming! I swear!)

ALANA ALBERTSON IS the former President of RWA's Contemporary Romance, Young Adult, and Chick Lit chapters. She holds a M.Ed. from Harvard and a BA in English from Stanford. She lives in San Diego, California, with her husband, two sons, and six rescue dogs. When she's not saving dogs from high kill shelters through her rescue Pugs N Roses, she can be found watching episodes of Cobra Kai, Younger, or Dallas Cowboys Cheerleaders: Making the Team.

Please join my newsletter to receive 2 free books!

Newsletter

Website

Email Me

Facebook Group